Joey The Seagull

by

Bard

DORRANCE
PUBLISHING CO
EST. 1920
PITTSBURGH, PENNSYLVANIA 15238

Dorrance Publishing Co
585 Alpha Drive
Pittsburgh, PA 15238
Visit our website at www.dorrancebookstore.com

ISBN: 979-8-88812-220-4
eISBN: 979-8-88812-720-9

Chapter One: Bro Beach

A beautiful sunny day at Bro Beach. A small beach town that's a little slice of paradise. The weather is always nice, there's a million outdoor activities to enjoy and wildlife is abundant. Among the wildlife are the seagulls. Joey Gull is a young seagull from a good family with honest values. He spends his days helping his uncle fish for the community, and his afternoons are filled with laid back fun at the beach with his friends.

Val, Jimmy and Sean have been friends with Joey since they were kids. Val's mother would watch them when they were little. These three friends gather items of trash from the beach waste baskets from the tourists, and then take them back to the community. It's an easy job, but they are not overly motivated and just like to catch the waves and lead that beach life.

Today, the seagulls hit the best waves in weeks. A great swell. They made their boards from lumber as children. They considered it one of their prized possessions. Synchronizing in perfect harmony, they catch each wave and go left and right, left and right, like a perfect dance. They do this multiple times, each time almost perfectly. They almost never falter, after all they do this every single day.

As the sun begins to set, they groove in from one last perfect wave. As they slide in from land, they hop off. They grab the boards and fly while laughing to the beach wall that separates the beach from public walkway. They lay the boards down in the sand and put their backs on the boards, facing the beach. Looking at a clear sky sunset, it's not something new at Bro Beach.

Val: Guy's, those waves were so gnarly!

Sean: Oh my God! What a rush! (He says with great enthusiasm).

Jimmy: Ha-ha, yeah best waves in weeks. We really killed it out there. We rock!!

Joey: Yeah, this is the life (He says very somberly). Hey guys you ever think like there is more to life? Like maybe, we were meant to do something more meaningful.

Sean: I don't think that much

Val: Yeah, thinking hurts my head (She says holding her head and swaying it back and forth).

Jimmy: What do mean Joey? The sun is shining, well setting now. Everyday it's always shining, though! Your Dad has set up this great community for all of us. What more could you want?

Joey: I don't know I just feel like I've reached a point in my life where I could do something different. There is a whole world out there, and I've never even left this beach town. Wouldn't you guys like to travel and broaden your horizons?

Sean: And miss the waves man... Never.

Val: Yeah, can't miss the waves, Joey.

Joey: Yeah, the waves are great, don't get me wrong. I just feel there is a whole world out there waiting to be seen. Waiting for me to make an impact. Change the world.

Sean: No, you're crazy; it's all the same.

Val: Yeah, stop making me think so much. The sun has almost set, I need to get back home.

Val and Sean grab their boards and fly off. Jimmy and Joey grab their boards, but before they fly off, Jimmy puts his wing on Joey's shoulder.

Jimmy: Joey, things are great here. Your father built this community years ago. All animals work together, and we help each other out. What else could you want. I mean someday you might even be the leader of this beach town.

Joey: I don't know jimmy, I just feel there is something out there, something more. I am not sure if there is anything worth seeing, but to not even try? I just want to know; I want to see the world in a different way. Do you understand?

Jimmy: I understand you feel unfulfilled. I do not feel the same way, but hey; to each their own. Maybe this will pass, maybe it's like a midlife crisis.

Joey: Gee Thanks

Jimmy: Oh, I'm just kidding, hey I got to go. See you tomorrow?

Joey: Yeah, I'll come by. I'll see you tomorrow, like always.

Joey and Jimmy Fly off home for the evening. Joey takes one last look at the beach. Joey sighs as the sun goes down and he returns home. He is ready for a meal his mother has made.

Chapter Two: Dinner With the Family

Joey arrives home to his mother finishing dinner. The family lives inside a church steeple in the center on the beach town. The top of the steeple is very high and overlooks the town from all directions. Inside is a modest setup with a kitchen/dining area and a few rooms. Sardines with Seaweed were on the menu this evening, a seagull favorite. Theresa Gull, Joey's mother, usually stays at home. She has very traditional values and loves to cook and keep up the house. She is a very loving mother but can be a bit of a nudge to Joey. She worries constantly about everything. She usually wears an apron even when not cooking, because "well you never know when you have to start cooking."

Joey's dad is late to dinner, again. This happens often, as Don Gull is always busy dealing with last minute issues that come up in the community. His father is a very humble man and does not show much emotion. He has a wisdom to him. He will ask questions but at times be short in conversation. It's not that he is trying to be rude, but more that he just has a lot on his mind. Joey comes through the window of the steeple and greets his mother.

Joey: Hey Mom

Theresa Gull: Joey! Joey! I'm so glad to see you. Please sit, sit down. Tell me how your day was. I'll get you a fish to taste! (She says with way too much excitement)

Joey: Mom, Mom I can wait for dinner (Joey says politely but with a little irritability).

Theresa Gull: Oh, OK Joey. I just don't know when your father will be home. You know he's late, working again as always.

Joey: I know he's busy Mom. I mean he runs the whole community, making sure everything is running right and fair.

Theresa Gull: I know, I just wish sometimes. You know?

Joey: I know Ma, I know.

Theresa Gull: So how was your day son? Did you do anything exciting?

Joey: No, I did the same thing I always do. Every day is the same. I wake up, I grab fish with Uncle Tony. Then I go surf and hang out by the beach.

Theresa Gull: Sounds like a good day

Joey: It was Ma, I just, I just don't know. I've been thinking of maybe taking a trip. Maybe moving away for a while. You know, see the world. Gain some other knowledge.

Joeys Mom drops a plate in shock. With a wide-eyed gaze says to her son in an overblown hysterical manner.

Theresa Gull: You are leaving home? Where will you go? What will you do? Who will make your meals for you?

Joey: Ma, Ma cool it down. I'm just thinking of a change.

Theresa Gull: Don't you tell me to cool down. My baby bird is leaving me. You know I only have one son, right?

Joey: Mom, I'm not your baby bird anymore, I'm a grown adult bird and I need to find my way!

Theresa Gull starts crying. Just as this happens Don Gull walks into the room. He looks tired and immediately looks at his wife, then at Joey, then back at his wife and then back Joey. Don Gull sighs and puts his wing over his head.

Don Gull: Ugh, what did you do Joey? Why is your mother upset?

Theresa Gull: He's, He's leaving us! (She says hysterically).

Joey: Ma! I was just thinking of going away and exploring new areas. Find some new opportunities. Meet somebody new. Maybe do a little soul searching to find myself.

Theresa Gull: Oh, like your uncle did? He came back and look how he is (she says angerly).

Don Gull: Alright both of you calm down! Ugh, it's been a long day. Can we calmly sit down and talk about this?

Theresa Gull: Dinners ready (she says a little calmer, but still with anger in her voice).

The table is already set, and Theresa brings the food out. There is a long pause before eating. Nothing is said for a while. Don Gull does a soft cough and begins to start conversation.

Don Gull: So, Joey what exactly are we talking about?

Joey: Dad, I just want to find my own way. Everything is the same here, every single day. There is a whole world out there. I have never seen any of it. I want to explore; I want to experience. Dad, I want to live.

Theresa Gull: You want to leave your family and friends. You want to leave everything behind you. (She cuts in angerly)

Don Gull: Easy my love! Let him speak.

Joey: I just want to do something different, before it's too late. I don't want life to pass me by.

Don Gull looks at his son and sees the sincerity in his face. He knows Joey needs a change. He puts down his fork and looks at his wife. He gives her a look that tells her to be calm. See slouches forward in her chair, as if to say I will not interrupt. Even though she really wants to.

Don Gull: How about this Joey, tomorrow you talk to Tony about what it's like beyond our beach town. He can give you some insight on how the world is outside the city. I could do it, but it would mean more coming from him. Then after fishing, you come to my office and see what I do each day. This will give you an idea of what the real world is like. After that, if you still feel passionate about leaving. We can discuss it further tomorrow during dinner.

Joey: I'll miss time with my friends if I see you dad. I might be late for surfing.

Don Gull: Yes, that will be a change. You need to make a small change, before you can make a very big one. Wouldn't you agree?

Joey: Yes, Dad. That makes a lot of sense.

They finish dinner quietly and Joey retires to his room. Don and Theresa head to the bedroom. They discuss the situation a little more. Theresa is a lot calmer now. They start a conversation quietly since Joey is in the next room.

Theresa Gull: So, are we really considering this.

Don Gull: Oh Theresa, everyone in this world needs to find their way in life. If this is what he needs to do to find himself, and to find peace with who he is, then who are we to get in the way of that.

Theresa Gull: But he's our baby, and you know what happened to my brother.

Don Gull: I know Theresa, Tony will talk to him tomorrow. Then he will see what I do, and maybe get more of a perspective about life.

Theresa Gull: Alright Dear, I guess we will see.

Meanwhile, Joey is in his room laying in his bed. He fantasizes about a life outside of his own. A world full of infinite possibilities, both good and bad. He is more excited to see Tony than ever before. He tosses and turns a little, knowing tomorrow is a big day. A day that could impact his life for the better or for the worse.

Chapter Three: Another Day of Fishing

The next morning Joey soars to the docks of the bay. This is where he usually meets up with his uncle Tony. They always meet at the same spot, a park bench overlooking the boating dock. From there they head to the bait dock where they meet a seal named Bob. Bob is always in the water, bobbing up and down. He gives advice on where the fish are gathering. Tony does not speak much but he always makes small talk with Bob every morning. After they get the advice from Bob, they take a few buckets and then catch fish for a few hours. They fish until they have a good amount to give to the community. Joey takes back the buckets to an enclosed rooftop by the beach, where numerous animals and his father work on community issues.

Today was no different than any other day, with the exception that Joey was going to have a real deep conversation with Tony. They pretty much never talk about anything except fishing. Tony helps the community out but is not involved actively. He never comes to the house for dinner and almost never talks to anybody but Joey and Bob. He does not have the warmest personality. Even if Tony wanted to warm up to others, it would not be well received. He has a huge scar and eye patch from an injury years ago. He never discusses it, and both of Joey's parents do not bring it up. Tony is the only one in the community to have left beach town and it is assumed that he encountered some tough times. Every time Joey had brought it up with his parents, they would give short answers and then quickly change the subject. They only thing he would consistently get from his mother was that "my younger brother was never the same when he came back from that city." Today was the day Joey was hopefully going to get some answers and maybe a few stories.

Joey flies to the bench where Tony is sitting. A somber grumpy face, as always. He is waiting for Joey with a few empty buckets for fish.

Joey: Hey Tony, great morning, isn't it?

Tony: Aww, it's ok. No different than any other day in this beach town.

Joey: You're always negative Tony. Be a little cheerier, would you.

Tony: Well the world is what it is, Joey.

Joey: I suppose, hey so I had a big conversation yesterday with my family.

Tony interrupts Joey quickly and tries to change the subject. This is something he did often when Joey tried to get personal.

Tony: We need to meet Bob before he leaves for the day.

They head to the bay bait spot where Bob hangs out. He's bobbing up and down next to the dock, like always.

Tony: Hey Bob, where are the fish swimming today?

Bob: Hey guys, out by the rocks today. There are tons of them, they are making their own waves. Should be a good day.

Tony: Thanks Bob, what would I do without you?

Bob: Not catch fish, Tony. You know that.

Tony and Bob always had a quick sarcastic blue-collar back and forth that Joey loved. He would try it on his friends, but they just wouldn't understand it. It is one of the many reasons Joey wanted to leave. No new experiences, no new conversations. Tony and Bob were clearly full of great years and experience. Though both didn't talk much, you could tell they were lifelong friends with years of different experiences. They had now become old souls. Joey always thought if he could ever get them to open up a little, they would have many stories to tell. They never really did though.

Tony: Alright Bob, I'll see you later in the day. Don't die on me.

Bob: I'm not that lucky, Tony.

Tony and Joey go to the rocks and start catching fish. Tony is amazing, he almost never misses. He also coaches Joey to catch them as well. Directing him on form and technique, telling him to always trust his instincts and never doubt his next moves. "When you doubt yourself, you have already given up your best performance." Tony would often say this when Joey failed at catching the fish.

Joey himself has become a great fisher, but he always takes pointers and advice. He knows Tony is the best, and any advice he gives to Joey, in the end, will make him a better fisher. They fly around in circles until they see the target, then they swoop down. They catch the fish in their mouths. Some of the other birds use their claws, but Tony always felt the mouth was the best strategy. "You can keep them from squirming around," Tony would say. They then place the fish into the bucket and repeat until the job is done.

After a few hours they catch four large buckets of fish and one small. The four buckets are for the community, the small bucket is for Bob and a few others around the docks. The idea is everyone gets a piece in return for other services. That's how the community works. When the buckets are full, they decide to take a break on the rocks. This is Joey's chance to break the ice and bring up the conversation.

Joey: Hey Tony, I got to talk to you about something. I'm thinking of leaving this beach town to find myself and have new experiences.

Tony changes his grumpy expression and seems generally concerned and confused. A look Joey has never seen before from Tony.

Tony: Why would you do that? Do your parents know?

Joey: Yes, they said to talk to you, and well, they said you might have some insight. You know, since you were gone for so long.

Tony: That was a very long time ago Joey. What exactly would you like to know?

Joey: What's it like Tony? Away from this town where everything always seems the same.

Tony: It's different, very different. The way others act and work together, it's not the same. I know things can be boring and mundane around here. Honestly, that can be a good thing. The world out there, it can be evil and rough. There is a lot less of the bad here at the beach, than there is in most places.

Joey: Is it that bad?

Tony: Not all of it, there are beautiful places and experiences everywhere. It made me see the world differently, some for better some for worse.

Joey: That's what I want. I want to see the world differently (he says with excitement).

Tony: I did too. That's why I left. I wanted to start a life of my own. When you do that, you can find out things about yourself. They might not all be good though. The world can change you. Someone who want's change will find it, but it might not be the change you desire. There are also some who might not want you to change whatever it is you want to change.

Joey: Wow, Tony that was deep, especially for you.

Tony: Yeah, I guess. So, Joey, when are you planning on going on this spiritual adventure?

Joey: Honestly tomorrow. If I don't do it now. Will I ever do it?

Tony: Ha, you sound like me when I was younger. Where will you go?

Joey: I've always been by the beach. I was thinking of going to the city. Maybe Angle city.

Tony: I spent time there, for a while. It's big, there is a lot going on. It's not the same as here.

Joey: What do you mean by that?

Tony: Not every place is like this beach town. Your Dad worked hard to make things the way they are today. It did not come easy, getting people to work together never is. Most animals in other areas do things for themselves and only themselves. Intentions of others are not always what you would think, others can be deceiving.

Joey: I know it's a challenge to go somewhere new and meet new people. I must do it though. Do you understand that?

Tony: I understand, your father will understand, but your mother? Let's just say there will be issues. She was not too keen on me leaving years ago.

Joey: Yeah, I know, I'm going to hear it tonight from her.

Tony: Yeah, but in the end, you must find your own way in life. Who knows maybe I'll visit you. If or when you get settled? If you do not meet me fishing tomorrow morning, should I assume you have left for this great adventure.

Joey: If you do not see me tomorrow, I'm gone. I guess you'll have to visit (Joey says with a smile).

Tony smiles back and gives Joey a half hug. This is more affection than Tony has probably ever given anyone. It throws Joey off a bit, but he likes it and they both flash a small smile. He hesitates for a second, but then asks the question he's wondered for years.

Joey: Hey Tony, what happened when you left. Nobody talks about it, and I can tell by the scars and patch on your eye. Clearly you have a past and a story to tell?

Tony gives a little smile and shakes his head. He stands up from the rocks that they were sitting on and stretches his wings. He smirks and looks at Joey.

Tony: Ask your mother at dinner and maybe she will tell you a little of it. I can't, I swore to your mother I would never speak of that to you. You can tell her

I said that too. I will leave you with this advice though. Always trust your instincts in every situation and..........

Joey finishes the sentence loudly as Tony takes off into the sky smiling as he has heard this hundreds of times.

Joey: When you doubt yourself, you have already given up your best performance!

Chapter Four: Take Your Son to Work Day

Joey soars through the bay and heads to the crowded beach. It's a very busy day. Humans are swarming the beach in large numbers. It's a little chaotic, but it can be good for the animals of the community. One man's trash can be an animal's treasure. Some animals are out scavenging for picnic leftovers, trash and water bottles. All those things and more, can help sustain a better life for the town.

Joey soars onto the rooftop where his father is usually giving orders to animals every day. Many animals are flying in and out for more than ten hours each day. He's at his desk looking frustrated as he always is.

Next to Don is his right-hand bird, Speedy. Speedy is a roadrunner. He takes orders that are needed and runs fast to deliver the messages. He does not fly, but he is lightning fast. He can deliver messages to others in minutes. Speedy is very high strung but great at his job. He always takes the orders and runs as fast as he can to deliver the news both big and small. Speedy talks very fast, except when he gives the exact orders. When he does this, he will mimic whoever told him to relay the message. It's an ongoing joke with the other animals that he does a great Don Gull impression. Though, he never shows Don the impression.

A few birds and some other animals are getting orders from Don when Joey lands on the rooftop. Only a handful of animals meet with Don. The ones that do though, they meet with him often.

Don Gull: Alright team, lets gather what we can out there. Squirrels, can we gather as much water from the inside of the houses as we can? You know we are in a drought, and we don't want to drink salt water.

Squirrels: Yes Sir!!!

Don Gull: Ok great, everyone else let's start gathering food and any unique materials we can use for building. Everyone needs at least a hut for shelter. Speedy, can give us some intel from some of the watchers on lookout?

Speedy: You got it Don! Hey Joey, can't talk now but I'm coming to dinner tonight.

Joey: Hey speedy!

Speedy zooms out of the building and the birds and other animals follow. Speedy is always dramatic with his exits and enters.

Joey: Well, that was a fast exit (Joey says jokingly, as he knows how Speedy is).

Don Gull: Yea, he is a real go getter.

Joey sits at the chair opposite to the desk of his father. Now that they are alone, he decides to ask him something he has always wondered.

Joey: Yeah, I know. So, dad, are you here every day just giving orders and solving problems. Don't you get stressed and burnt out?

Don Gull: Very much so Joey, but someone must do it and I have been doing it for a very long time.

Joey: Do you ever think of quitting?

Don Gull: Yes, I have many times thought of giving up. However, if the person at the top leaves without a good exit strategy, everything this town has built could be lost for all the animals. We have a good thing going here.

Joey: So, you sacrifice for others?

Don Gull: Yes, for the greater good.

Joey: What was it like here at the beach. You know, before this system was all built up?

Don Gull: It was chaos, every animal was in it for themselves. There was no order. Food and water were sometimes hard to sustain, and some animals would turn on each other to survive. It was very different and much harder to survive for everyone. You see Joey, for a society to work you need some basic guidelines and understanding from everyone involved. There are three basic needs to life food, shelter and most importantly fresh water.

Joey: How did you ensure that everyone could get those three things?

Don Gull: It did not come easy. We had to make sure that everyone had their share. Doing that required teamwork, teamwork from everyone. All animals had to play a part. Many animals scavenge for leftover food from the trash. Others help with providing basic shelter by gathering materials. We provide shelter on rooftops and other areas where there are not too many humans. Birds transport water from fresh water sources and some, like you Joey, they fish. When we work as a team, we can all accomplish more of our individual goals. When we do it by ourselves, we can become overwhelmed with what is on our plate for survival.

Joey: Was it easy to bring everyone together like that?

Don Gull: No not at all. Many resisted; it took a lot of blood, sweat and tears to accomplish this. That's my biggest concern about you leaving. It's not like this in other areas.

Joey: I know Dad, but I have skills to survive. I'm tough! (Joey flexes his wings).

Don Gull: I know you have the skills. That is why you have my blessing, if it is something you want to do.

Joey: Thanks Dad (Joey says with a sincere smile), I think it is something I need to do.

Speedy runs into the room very quickly.

Speedy: Sorry to interrupt, Ivan the Crow says, "Tell Don everything here is looking good today, no one is slacking off." (Speedy makes an impression of the Crow as he does with many others when repeating words, Joey Laughs at the Impersonation).

Don Gull: What would I do without you Speedy?

Speedy: Go a lot slower sir (Speedy smiles).

Suddenly a bunch of animals come in saying they need Don's advice on some shelter plans. Joey feels he should exit so his dad can do his Job.

Joey: Dad great talking to you, I'll see you tonight to discuss more.

Don Gull: Sounds good Son, Alright guys what's the issue this time.

Joey exits the rooftop and starts to fly off to the beach to see his friends He is late for the first time ever. He wants to say goodbye to them before dinner. He has officially made up his mind that he is leaving tomorrow. He is very worried about how his friends will take it. It's a somber flight to the beach. He spends the time thinking of how he is going to tell them this news.

Chapter Five: Last Hangout with The Gang

Joey soars to the beach and sees his friends perched up to beach sidewalk sideway with the surfboards stuck into the sand. They are clearly done with surfing. Joey glides in to greet them. They look upset.

Joey: Hey Guys! How were the waves?

Val: Terrible! Also, our good friend ditched us.

Joey: Val it's not like that, I was talking with my father.

Sean: Yeah whatever, dude.

They are all clearly upset with him, even Jimmy who is the more understanding one. Joey knows he needs to lighten the mood before he drops the big news that he is going away for a while. He decides to suggest a little game of Target Practice.

Joey: I'm sorry guys, but hey since I missed surfing. What do you say we play a game of target practice? You know, for old times' sake. It will be fun.

Sean: Oh my God! We have not played that in forever

Val: Oh yeah!!! This is going to be good. I see a lot of nice cars.

Jimmy smiles at Joey as he knows what he is doing. He is lightening the mood with others. He has a feeling Joey might have something to say after the game.

Jimmy: Let's do it guys, this will be fun.

Target Practice is a game they used to play all the time when they were younger. What they would do is find some of the nicer cars, usually by a nice restaurant by the beach. Fine Dining with a View, FDV Bistro for short. That was the name of the popular restaurant that was always busy. When a car would leave the parking lot, they would wait for it to exit. Then they would fly over the car, and poop on it. Depending on where the poop landed, they would get points.

The rules of the game were simple and listed below:

They would find three cars during the game

Each player would fly separately and attempt to poop on the car.

The front of the car and rear trunk is worth a point.

The top hood of the car is worth two points.

The Windshield is a bullseye, and worth three points.

The best score is nine points and after three times the player with the best score wins.

If there is a tie; the two highest scores would have a sudden death showdown to see who was the winner.

They perched up on the restaurant rooftop and waited for the first car to exit. They were all filled with excitement and glee. A great childlike rush of adrenaline ran through them. Especially Val, who always loved the game. Joey was almost always the winner, since his fishing skills lined up similar to the game. Suddenly, a green Porsche comes out of the driveway. The eyes of each one of them grew large and smiles ran from ear to ear.

Sean: Hey guys, check that one out! That's our first victim. I'll go first!

Sean soars through the air and squints one eye; he then lands a good-sized turd right on the front of the car.

Sean: Hey not bad, I got to get the rust off.

Jimmy then flies in ahead of the car and he lands one on the front as well.

Jimmy: Right back at you Sean.

Val flies effortlessly, not stopping her speed. With a huge smile, she lands one right on the driver's side of the windshield. The car stops for a second, the man rolls down the window to look up and is obviously frustrated.

The car begins to move again and now it's Joey's turn. Joey circles around the car, like how he fishes. After a few circles he lands one right in the dead center middle of the windshield. They all laugh uncontrollably back to the rooftop. A shout can be heard by the driver saying, "stupid birds!!"

The Score
Jimmy – 1
Sean – 1
Val – 3
Joey – 3

Next comes a brown BMW rolling out of the parking lot.

Sean: Oh yeah, this is my shot at redemption.

Sean flies back out and squints the other eye this time. This time he got it, right side of the windshield. Jimmy, Val and Joey all hit the windshield as well. The car speeds off frustrated. There is four different splatted white poop marks, all in almost a perfect square. The windshield wipers and fluid does almost nothing to clean it. They are all laughing hysterically as they fly back for a second time.

Jimmy: looks like we all got our groove back.

Val: We sure did!! (She says with a gleeful smile and laugh)

The Score
Jimmy – 4
Sean – 4
Val – 6
Joey – 6

Finally, a yellow McLaren starts to move out of the parking lot. They have never seen this nice of a car.

Sean: Guys, look at that thing!

Val: Wow, oh I'm going to enjoy this. I just ate half a burrito for lunch.

The McLaren's going fast, right out of the lot. Almost as if the driver knows what is coming.

Jimmy: Oh, this will be challenging, we need to hurry.

Sean soars as fast as he can and drops one on the front of the car for a point.

Sean: Not bad, it's going fast. You guys might have a hard time hitting it.

Jimmy flies straight past the car and anticipates where the car will be. He hits the back of the car for a point.

Jimmy: you really have to get in front of the car, it is going so fast.

Val speeds by the car and drops one right in the middle of the windshield while screaming bombs away!! She is cheerful with great pride. "Yeah Val!" They all scream. She smiles, not saying anything, but is obviously very proud of herself.

The car slows down a bit after the hit. It is Joey's turn.

Sean: Val if he misses, you are the winner. If he hits, you are both going to sudden death overtime.

Val: Yeah, but Joey almost never misses. The car has also slowed down.

Joey circles the car and moves in on the target. He's confident he's got it. He then looks back at his friends who have already returned to the rooftop. He looks at them and sees the great time they are having, and smiles on each of their faces. He realizes that when he goes away, he is really going to miss them. He then realizes that he shouldn't win. Joey is about to give them some tough news that will upset them. He doesn't want to be the winner before he does that. Joey waits two extra seconds than he normally would and lets it go. It's dead center but the car just passes by and the poop splatters on the street. He does not hit the car at all.

Sean: Wow, Joey never misses! Val is the winner!

The Final Score
Jimmy – 5
Sean – 5
Val – 9
Joey – 6

Joey soars back to the rooftop, he missed but has a smile on his face. They all give congrats and a high fives to Val, who is still very excited about the win.

Val: How did you miss?

Joey: I thought the car was going to slow down again. Congratulations Val, that was a great game. You were really on it today.

Val: I rock!! (She says with her wings held high as she dances in circles).

Jimmy: Yeah, you sure do. (Jimmy says smiling, while laughing at her victory dance).

They fly back to the surf boards, laughing all the way. They start talking about how fun the game was, and how it brought them back to the good old days. They sit back down tired from game. Joey knows this is the perfect time to address his friends that he is leaving. He knows it's going to be a tough conversation.

Joey: Guys, that was a great time. I always have a great time every day I am with all of you. I love all of you so much. I have some news though.

The smiles run away from his friends faces, as if they know what is coming. They all sigh a little.

Joey: I'm leaving tomorrow. I'm going to check out Angle City. I don't know when I'll be back, it could be a while.

Jimmy: Yeah, we kind of thought you were going to say that today.

Sean: When will you be back, Bro.

Joey: I don't know, but I will come back. This isn't forever.

Sean: What about the surf? Won't you miss it?

Joey: Yeah, I will miss surfing, fishing with my uncle and my family. I just need to do this. I need a change for a while.

Sean: I'll miss you too Joey.

Val is silent. She is clearly upset. Val has always not been able to adapt to change and this is a big one. Joey feels the need to comfort her. She can be sensitive, and this is big news.

Joey: Val, I'll miss you too.

Val: I know, I just don't want things to change. I like what we all have here.

Joey: There will always be changes, but the one thing that will never change is that all of you will always be my friends. Nothing will change that. I will always visit, and you can visit me.

Val: Alright, I'll miss you. Even though you are no longer the best at target practice. (She smiles).

Joey hugs Sean and Val. It's very somber and tearful. They then grab the surfboards and fly home. It is just Jimmy and Joey now. Jimmy looks like he has something to say.

Jimmy: You know you are my best friend, right?

Joey: I know Jimmy, you are mine too. I just need to do this.

Jimmy: I know you do. I've known for a long time you needed something more in life. You are like your father, always wanting to make yourself and people around you better.

Joey: Thanks, Jimmy. That might be the kindest thing anyone has ever said to me.

Jimmy: I mean it and hey, I know you missed on purpose in the game.

Joey smiles and doesn't say anything. There is a small silence and Joey hugs Jimmy.

Joey: We will always be friends.

Jimmy: I know, just do me a favor. Never change who you are. Others around you will always try to change you in life. You are a well-rounded, caring and kind person. Whatever you get into in this the world, do not let that go. Promise me that, will you?

Joey: I promise Jimmy

Jimmy soars off with his board and Joey stays back. He looks at the beach one more time. He looks at a few animals finishing up the day, a few little ones playing by the beach, some humans are packing up some towels. He gets emotional for a minute and flies away. He takes the long way home to gather his thoughts. This has been a long and exhausting day, and it is not over yet. Joey still needs to talk to his mother, and he knows she is going to be upset.

Chapter Six: The Last Supper

After a good hour of flying around the town and thinking. Joey comes home to see dinner is already on the table. This is a rare occurrence. It's a feast of fishes, way too much food. The food is all laid out, ready to be eaten. His father and Speedy are already at the table. There is a red backpack sitting at the chair where Joey usually sits. Joey walks in slowly and begins to greet the family. His mother is already at the table.

Joey: What is this?

Theresa Gull: That is your backpack, for your long trip. I am packing you a goody bag.

Joey: Goody bag? We were going to talk about me leaving I thought.

Theresa takes a deep sigh and looks at Joey with a soft accepting smile. An unexpected look that sets Joey back a bit.

Theresa Gull: I already know the answer. Val's mother spoke to me after talking to Val. Word travels fast at the beach, you know that.

Joey looks at all of them and sees acceptance on both his parents face. Speedy grins with a proud look and shakes his head, as to say everything's alright.

Speedy: I respect you for making this journey. It takes great courage.

Joey: Thank you, Speedy (Joey says somberly).

Theresa Gull: Joey, I love you. Promise me this, you will always be safe and make good choices.

Joey: I will Mom.

They begin to feast on the food. It is a wonderful feast with all kinds of fish. Speedy eats so much his belly is bulging out. They laugh and talk about old times, funny occurrences and about what they remember about Joey as a kid. Theresa Gull packs a few waters and fish in the backpack.

Theresa Gull: I hope this isn't too heavy. I didn't want you to be hungry on the long trip. The backpack can be used for storing essentials and food on your journey.

Joey: Thanks Mom, I really appreciate it. Are you ok with this?

Theresa Gull: Not really, but I've accepted it. I just want my baby to be happy. Just don't ever change who you are.

Joey smiles and hugs his mom. She is a little teary but has come to terms with everything. Clearly there was a talk while Joey was flying around. Don Gull probably emphasized having a happy last evening together.

Speedy: This is a very touching moment. (Speedy interrupts uncomfortably during the touching moment).

Don Gull: Speedy...

Don Gull looks at his son with a sense of pride. He sees a little of himself in Joey.

Don Gull: My boy is a man, and he will pave his own way.

Joey: Thanks Dad, do you have any advice?

Don Gull: The Sun rises in the East and sets in the West. You will always find where you need to go by looking at the sun. Angle city is North of here. The Ocean is always to the West. The Desert is to the East, and Our Home will always be South, and it will always be here for you; if and when you need it.

Joey: That's great advice. Anything else?

Don Gull: Always surround yourself with people who are good natured and want the same things. You already know those type of people.

Speedy: And run really fast if you see trouble!!

Speedy runs around the table several times and everyone chuckles.

Joey: Oh, Speedy I'll miss you.

Theresa Gull: As much as I do not want this night to end. You have a big day tomorrow.

Joey: I know I love you all

Joey hugs everyone at the table. His mother, he hugs a few times. He knows this is hard on her. He then goes to his room, and unlike the night before; he falls asleep right away. He had a long emotional day, and tomorrow will be a long one.

Speedy begins to leave and Don Gull grabs his shoulder. Both Don and Theresa look at him with a stern gaze.

Theresa Gull: Speedy we have a favor to ask.

Don Gull: I want to ask you to keep an eye on our son. Every few days with your speed, you can race back and forth; to see how he is doing.

Speedy: Who will report all your daily information when I do this?

Don Gull: Ivan the Crow can handle it the days you are not here.

Speedy: OK, but he is not as fast; and his impersonation of you is terrible.

Don Gull: We'll make do the days you are not here Speedy. (Don says chuckling) Will you do this for Theresa and me, this would mean a lot?

Speedy: You guys are like family. Of course I will.

Speedy shoots out of the Gulls home. Don and Theresa begin to retire for the evening. They peak into Joey's room and smile at their child who is sleeping comfortably, hugging his pillow.

Theresa: I'm going to miss our little boy.

Don Gull: Me too Theresa, me too. He will make the right decisions. We raised him the right way.

Chapter Seven: The Journey Begins

Joey soars through the air with his red backpack strapped to each shoulder. A big smile on his face. He is filled with excitement, fear and adrenaline as he exits the beach town for the first time in his life. He starts going North to neighboring beach towns. The stimulation from all the new sceneries is breathtaking. The sky is clear, and the day is warm. He witnesses mountain tops for the first time and decides to head east for a little bit to experience the breathtaking views. They are beautiful.

Joey takes a break on a mountain top and looks southwest. "I wonder how far I have traveled? I wonder if I can still see Bro Beach?" It's about mid-day and it is much warmer than he is used to. He has been flying along the mountains and desert for hours. Checking out the new and interesting places. He has already gone through half of his water, and he hasn't seen any sources of water where he can refill his bottles. He continues to fly further north. As the day comes to an end, Joey eventually gets tired and flies high up on a mountain top.

The sun begins to set, and he decides to stay in a tree on a mountain with a view. He finds a cozy spot where he can sleep for the night and eats a fish. He had a feeling that the first day was going to be exciting, but tough. Joey has always been very social, and he has never had a day where he does not talk to anyone at all. He finds it a little lonely. A wolf howls in the distance, spooking Joey at first. He knows he is safe in the tree, but these strange new noises are foreign to him. Thoughts of doubt cloud Joey's mind, and he begins to ponder questions to himself. Was this the right decision? Am I cut out for this? Is this what I really want? Joey assures himself that this is what he wants. Then slowly falls asleep. He flew more today than he has ever flown before. It was hot outside, much warmer than he expected or experienced before. Tomorrow is another day. As the sun sets, he closes his eyes; the first time he has done this away from his family.

Joey wakes to a rising sun flashing in his eyes. It's a little earlier than he is used to waking up. He rubs his eyes and sits up. He eats another fish and drinks some water. Today, the plan is to go north through the mountains and find some more water.

He flies through the lower mountains, after about an hour or two; he finds a nice stream with trees. It is a breathtaking quiet and serene area. He drinks the rest of his water and fills up all the bottles he has. After filling up, he drinks as much as he can from the stream until he can't drink anymore. He is going to take a deeper look into the desert today. He knows finding water could be an issue.

As Joey finishes drinking the water from the stream, he looks around. "Wow this would not be a bad place to survive," he says to himself. There is beautiful scenery, a large cave opening for shelter and a water source. The water looks a little low because of the drought, and he does not see too many fish. There is life here though. He sees insects, some fruit bushes and tall grass. He thinks to himself, if I was just trying to survive just by myself and get by; this would be the perfect place to do so. It is a little Oasis. Joey makes a mental note of where this place is located. It's a great place to visit between the city and his beach town. He then put's everything in his backpack and continues with his journey.

After a few hours he travels Northeast to the desert area. The area is flat and very hot. There is vegetation but only low bushes. As he flies, Joey begins to see a large animal in a bush. His curiosity makes him circle back and forth. Joey is trying to identify what it is below. As Joey gets closer, a white and black creature runs fast out of the bushes. The creature runs aggressively fast, and Joey follows it; trying to figure out what the creature is. Then very suddenly, the creature drops lifelessly on the ground. Joey is confused and worried, is the creature, ok? Should he help? He flies to the ground near the lifeless body and while circling close to it, he realizes it's a possum. They have a few in the community at home. As Joey lands on the ground, the possum jumps up and screams. Startled by the action, Joey jumps backwards. In a loud screeching voice, the possum screams at the top of his lungs, "I'll Kill You!!!"

Chapter Eight: A Family Encounter

Joey falls back on his butt and sticks his wings out as a sign of peace. Startled, he screams back in a defensive way, alerting the possum of peace.

Joey: I do not mean you any harm, I was just seeing if you were ok.

Possum: Oh, well then. It is very nice to meet you. (He says calmly).

The possum quickly changes his tone rather surprisingly. Joey is still a little startled and turns his head towards the bush that the possum came out of. He sees in the bush another possum, along with two small young possums. It's a family. Joey realizes the possum was trying to protect his family. The fact that Joey was circling around in flight, most likely looked like a threat to the family. Joey stands up, brushes himself off and then addresses the Possum. The rest of the family slowly emerges out of the bushes.

Joey: Nice to meet you. I'm sorry, I realize I might of gave off the wrong impression. My name is Joey and I'm just passing by.

Peter: Oh, so are we. Well my name is Peter and that's Mary. These are our two children, Pip and Nip.

Joey looks at the rest of the family slowly creeping out of the bushes, he notices they are still a little timid. Mary has the children close next to her. The two kids slowly jump off the mothers back and waddle around. Joey notices that both kids have only three legs. They move surprisingly well for not having the additional leg. Thrusting the hind legs forward and using the front leg as a peg to balance, they move with surprising grace. He then softly and in a non-threating manner addresses the others.

Joey: Hi, nice to meet you all. My name is Joey.

Pip and Nip: Hello stranger!! (They say in a high-pitched voice standing on two legs and waving the arm that they have).

Mary: Hi Joey

Joey: So where are you all headed? It's awfully hot and dry in this area.

Peter: We don't know, we are just trying to survive. It's hard for us to get around with the little ones. Food and water are hard to come by.

Joey looks at the family and empathizes with the situation they are in. He knows that his ability to fly is a great advantage for finding food and water. They do not have that ability. They are not only dealing with children, but children with a disadvantage for moving around. He takes off his backpack and removes a fish and a bottle of water. He hands it to Peter.

Joey: I have some food and water. Do you like fish?

Mary: Oh, we can't take that (she says with a sense of pride).

Joey: No please do, there is nothing around for a few miles. I have more in my backpack. I can go back to where I came from and refill again.

Peter: Thank you kind sir, this is the nicest gesture anyone has ever done for us. It's been hard for us lately. The drought has caused us to migrate, looking for a good place to survive.

The possums all start eating the fish and drinking the water. They eat it quickly, then all take turns drinking the water. Both are finished very quickly. The sun is slowly setting. Joey realizes what he gave was not enough. He takes the rest of his fish and water out and offers the rest. He also fears that the family will not survive in the desert, but how can he help? Joey then has a great Idea. The Oasis!

Joey: Listen, I have an idea. You all seem like kind souls, and I would like to offer to share the rest of my fish and water with you. I also would like to guide you to a place I found, it's a little up the mountain.

It has trees, a stream and fruit. There is a lot of bugs though.

Peter: Bugs!! You hear that kids? This place has bugs and fruit!

Pip and Nip: We love bugs!! (They do a little hopping dance that is very cute)

Joey smiles and lays the rest of the fish and water out. They all feast and while they eat, Joey discusses the plan.

Joey: So, here is my plan. I will head southwest back to the area and grab some fruit and water. While I do this, you can start making your way to the Oasis. It's southwest of here.

Peter: Southwest? How will I know which way to go?

Joey suddenly realizes that he needs to explain navigating the sun to Peter. Joey goes in detail to all the possums on how to determine where to go. The same way his father told him, just before he left. A sense of pride goes through Joey, knowing he is passing the knowledge he has learned to help others. The family is excited and now very full from the large meal. The mother takes the children to bed under the bush. There is now moonlight and Peter humbly looks at Joey to address him.

Peter: Joey I am so grateful for you helping us. Why are you doing this?

Joey: Because it's the right thing to do. When we help each other, the world is a better place. Everyone in the end is better for it.

Peter: That's a good motto to live by. You must have been raised right. I hope we can instill that on our children.

Joey smiles at the thought of his family teaching him the right way to go about life.

Joey: Yes, I was raised by thoughtful and caring friends and family.

Joey looks at Peters family in the bushes and wants to ask about the children's deformed leg. He pauses for a quick second, but then decides to ask.

Joey: Peter there is something I want to ask you. If I am out of line, please no hard feelings. How did your children hurt their legs?

Peter: Well, they were born like that. When Mary gave birth, we noticed the missing limb. It's been hard when traveling, but they are so happy and positive. They do not know any other way.

Joey empathizes with not only the kids, but also Peter and Mary. He thinks of how hard it would be to always be on the move while caring for young children.

Joey: Do you get frustrated?

Peter: All the time. They are always so positive; I can't show my frustrations. They get better at adjusting every day. They can hunt for bugs in the sand and are very smart. They sometimes can spot something in the distance that Mary and myself haven't seen yet. They rely on their other abilities to compensate for not being as mobile as they could be.

Joey: Almost like superhero powers. (Joey smiles)

Peter: In some ways yes. (Peter smiles back) You could say they have adapted to what they can and can't do. Evolved out of necessity to the environments we are exposed to.

Joey: I guess we all do that to point.

Peter: Yes, we do. We grow and evolve as animals; it's a part of life. We will continue to grow and adapt to our surroundings. It's part of survival.

Joey: I suppose it is. I wish everyone on the earth would just work together. The world would be a better place.

Peter: It would, but you must understand that not everyone has your outlook on life. There are many who struggle and have been hurt by others. After getting hurt so many times, you start to distrust others. It's one of the reasons we move alone. It's also the reason I got defensive when I saw you circling around us.

Joey: That's why you played dead?

Peter: Yes, that's why I played dead. There may be a time when you will need to surprise a threat with acting weak. Sometimes we must act weak when we are strong, and strong when we are weak. The element of surprise can be a powerful tool. Most of us believe what we see and see what we hope for.

Joey: Wow, that's deep Peter.

Peter: I have my moments (he smiles and then yawns). Well, that is enough late night talking for one evening. We have a long trip tomorrow. I need to play dead for myself for a few hours.

Peter walks back to the bush with his family. Then right before settling down he looks back at Joey. With small smile and approving nod, he addresses Joey one last time.

Peter: Hey Joey, thank you again for what you are doing for my family. You are one of a kind.

Joey smiles and says nothing back. There is nothing to say. He is just doing what he thinks is right. He falls asleep quickly on the desert ground. Knowing tomorrow is a different day than what he had planned.

In the distance there is a small animal overlooking the family and Joey. He has been watching the whole time. The animal perks up from the dark bush. It's a roadrunner. It's Speedy checking on Joey. "He's doing alright, his dad would be proud." Speedy then runs back in the direction of Bro Beach.

Chapter Nine: Helping Out

Joey wakes to the sun rising with no clouds in the sky. He yawns and hears noise in the background. The kids are already up and playing in the sand. The parents are slowly moving around, as it is clear they have also just awoken from the night slumber. Joey greets everyone with a good morning and then begins to head back to where he came from to the mountain oasis. He gives one last lesson to the family about how to navigate. Then flies back to mountains to grab water and food and meet them on their ground journey.

Joey's kindness does come at a price. He is detouring his trip for a few days to help. It's also much harder to survive when suppling food and water to a family that moves slow. He arrives at the oasis he was at previously. It still looks like a perfect place for the family to make a home. An abundance of food, shelter and water.

Joey begins drinking water from the stream. Then he begins refilling the bottles and putting them in his red backpack. He starts looking for fish in the streams. He sees very few fish. The water is very low from the drought but there are a few deep spots in the streams. He circles around the water and is able to catch a few small trout. Joey eats one and does not like the fish that much. It's his first time eating a freshwater fish. The fish taste a lot less "salty" than the ocean fish he is used to eating.

After putting a few fish back in the water. He looks at a berry bush and begins picking them. He tries one. "Eh not bad," Joey says, "I think the possums like berries and bugs." He looks at the basin of the stream and sees a bunch of bugs.

"Gross, I don't want those in my bag." He picks some more berries and then takes off to the desert trying to find the family.

Joey starts flying, looking at the lower mountain areas. It's hot and dry. The family is nowhere to be found. He begins to get frustrated. "Where are they?" he mutters with great frustration. "Are they that slow?" Joey begins going further down the mountain and is at the bottom where the desert begins. He sees the family moving, but slowly.

Joey had anticipated that they would be slow. At the rate they are going, they will be even slower going up the mountain. He anticipated maybe two days at most. However, given the immobility of the children and the parents carrying them up the mountain. The time will probably take maybe four days at this rate.

Joey comes up with a plan to take the children on his back and then wait for the parents. That way they can move faster without the kids. It should take off a day of travel, maybe two. The only issue is how will the family take this. It took them a while to warm up to Joey, now he is going to take the children. Joey understands how this advice could be taken with doubt, but in reality; it's the safest and most efficient way to get them to the oasis.

Joey flies down and greets the family.

Pip and Nip: Joey!!!

Joey: Hey everyone, I have some food and water.

They all sit on a large rock at the base of the mountain and have some food and water. The terrain is much rockier at the bottom of the mountain. The family looks tired and dehydrated. The heat was rough for Joey, he can only imagine what it must be like for a family on the hot ground. Joey at least has a breeze in the air when he flies around.

Joey: So, how are you guys doing?

Mary: We are exhausted from carrying the kids on our back in this heat. That rocky hill sure looks like a challenge. We usually stay on ground away from the hills.

Joey: Yeah, about that. I think I have an idea to have this trip go a little easier.

Peter: What's the plan Joey? You are full of ideas.

Joey: I think I should take the children to the oasis. It's not that far for me. At this rate, all of you will be traveling twice as long. I know we just met yesterday, but me taking the kids seems like the best solution to the problem.

Mary: I don't know, we have never let our children out of our sight.

Joey: I understand this is a leap of faith, but with those rocks and you climbing them with the children; there might not be another option. I really think....

Peter interrupts Joey and has a stern look on his face.

Peter: Joey that's enough. Mary can I speak with you for a minute?

Peter and Mary walk a good twenty feet away from Joey and the kids. They discuss amongst themselves for a while. Joey can see it is an intense conversation, but he cannot hear what they are saying. The kids are playing on the rock. They are trying to climb higher parts of rock and giggling as they fall. Joey smiles and says to them "hey guys, be careful." They tip over on their backs and laugh uncontrollably. They are having a good time and don't seem to be worried about anything. On the other hand, Peter and Mary are still in a heated conversation. Both talking over each other at times and giving multiple facial expressions.

Peter: Joey come over here. (He says loudly, as if the news is urgent)

Joey slowly walks over to them, and Peters voice goes down a little as to make sure the children cannot hear what he is about to say. Even if they could, they were playing and wouldn't be listening. It is clear to Joey that Peter and Mary want to have an intense conversation.

Peter: Are we friends, Joey?

Joey looks perplexed at the question and gives an inquisitive look. He then looks at Mary and see's she is very concerned. He then realizes something, it's not Peter he needs to convince; it's Mary.

Joey: Yes, after last night's deep conversation; I consider us friends. Peter, do you consider me a friend?

Peter: You can call me Pete. My friends and family call me Pete. Can I call you Joe?

Joey had never been called Joe. It seemed more grown up; he didn't hate it. It sounded like his father's name being shortened from Donald to Don.

Joey: You can call me Joe. I've never had a nickname before, Pete. (He says with a smile).

Peter: Sometimes good friends, lifetime friends, what they do is, they give each other nicknames. Lifetime friends trust their lives and the lives of their families with each other. Would we be able to trust our family with you?

Joey looks at Mary and sees she really needs convincing. He stops addressing Peter and looks Mary strait in the eye with a serious face. The tone of his voice is like he is swearing to God in a courtroom.

Joey: Pete (he says looking at Mary), you can trust me with your family. I would also trust you with my family.

Mary looks at Peter and she nods with approval. Mary speaks with still a little doubt in her voice.

Mary: What if something happens to us while you have the children?

Joey: I will fly back home and bring them to my mother. She always wanted more children. That's not going to happen though. The trip will be easier if you don't carry the children.

Mary looks Joey in the eyes with a sense of relief. She then looks at Peter and gives another nod of approval. It's settled with no words. They make way back to the rock where the children are still playing. Mary addresses the children.

Mary: Hey Pip and Nip, how would you like to go on a trip with Uncle Joe tomorrow?

Pip and Nip: Yes, yes, yes! Will we fly?

They both try to fly with the leg and stump and fall over. Everyone else can't help but chuckle at how cute they looked.

Mary: Yes, you will fly to a special place. Then have all the food and water you could ever want. Then mommy and daddy will be by later tomorrow or the next day. Would that be, ok?

Pip and Nip: Sleepover!!!

Mary looks at Peter and Joey. She then smiles and shrugs her shoulders. She now seems a little less worried.

Mary: Well, they don't care. I guess we will give this a shot.

Peter: Alright kids, it's settled. Tomorrow you are flying with Uncle Joey.

Pip and Nip: Yay, this will be fun!

They begin to settle down for the night. All of them sleeping near the big rock. Everyone is exhausted from the traveling. Mary sings a soft lullaby to the children. It starts to even put Joey and Peter to sleep.

Joey: That was beautiful, Mary.

Mary: Thanks, my mom sang it to me.

Chapter Ten: The Babysitter

The next morning everyone is up a little early before the sun rises. Mary is spending a little time with the children and trying to get her time in; before the separation anxiety of not being around the children kicks in. Peter is stretching on the rock, getting ready for the big climb. After this they all take a little time for breakfast. The possums eat the berries.

Peter: Joe, you don't like berries?

Joey: I've never had them; they do not look appetizing.

Joey tried a berry yesterday but decided to let Peter introduce them. The look on Peters face gave Joey the impression Peter wanted to give Joey some experience for helping.

Peter: Here give one a try, they are good for you. They give you lots of energy.

Joey takes a berry and throws it up in the air and catches it in his mouth. He swishes it in his mouth, almost like he's sipping a glass of wine. Then he smacks his lips together and makes a taste sound.

Joey: Hmm, not bad. It's better than the freshwater fish. I'll have some more when I get back. Kid's we will have a berry party!

Pip and Nip: Berry party!!! With bugs!!!

Joey: Gross, not for me. (He says with a dissatisfied face).

Pip and Nip: We will find you some! You will like it.

Mary: Now kids berry's might be good for Joey, but bugs are not for everyone.

Joey: Maybe kids, if you behave, I will try one with you tonight.

Joey smiles and then looks at the parents and begins to grab his backpack and offer it to them.

Joey: Take this bag with food and water for the trip. Please, it will keep you hydrated.

Peter: No, we can't, it's too heavy. Plus, the children can safely go in the bag while you fly.

Joey: Wow, Peter you are the one with the ideas now.

Peter: It's Pete, remember Joe?

Joey: Sorry Pete. Bye Mary, they are going to be ok.

Mary hugs Joey and whispers "please take care of them." She then addresses the kids, telling them to behave for Uncle Joey. She has some tears in her eyes and places the kids in the backpack.

Joey hands them each a bottle of water with some berries in them. This should hold them over on the trip. He then flies up in the air and circles around the parents. The parents waving at them saying goodbye. The children are screaming bye to the parents, along with "we are flying, we are flying!" The parents grab the bottles of water in their mouths and scatter up the mountain. Shortly after, they are both out of sight and Joey begins to fly faster and faster. The kids are filled with joy, excitement and wonder as they go through the air. Both little heads sticking out of the backpack with huge smiles on their faces.

They arrive at the oasis a little later than expected. Joey's back is sore from the flight. There was some food, half-filled water bottles and two children in his backpack. He also was flying more carefully since he knew he was carrying children. Not to mention the dry heat was terrible. "That was harder than expected," he says landing at the oasis. He puts the children down and jumps in the water to cool off. It feels great, like when he would wipe out on the surfboard on a warm day and just stay in the water for a bit. He exits the stream to see the kids have walked over to the water to cool themselves off.

Pip and Nip: We are just like Uncle Joey!!

Joey smiles at the scene. He remembers mimicking his uncle fishing when he was a young gull. "We really are not that much different," he says to himself. Then as they walk out of the water together, suddenly Pip and Nip stop.

Pip and Nip: Shhhhhh

They both crouch low and start to crawl. They see a spot in the ground and start to dig; they then stick their noses into the sand. Their heads are almost completely buried and suddenly they jump up with their hind legs and pop out of the ground; almost doing a complete flip.

Joey: What in the world was that?

Pip and Nip both open their mouths to show a huge grub and start to gobble it down. Joey is very impressed by this.

Joey: Wow you guys are talented. How did you know they were in the spot in the ground?

Pip: We can sense it

Nip: Yeah, it's a special power

Joey then remembers what Pete had said to him. How they can compensate for what they don't have by being more efficient in other areas of life. Seeing it live and firsthand; made Joey believe in this more. How we adapt to survive is different depending on our situation.

Joey: You guys sure do have your talents. How about we get in the shade in that small cave over there.

The kids follow Joey into the cave, and they lay down together. Both nestled under each wing. The cave is much cooler, and they fall asleep early. Joey had hoped that the parents would have made it back by now. He knew it would probably be in the morning or midday tomorrow but had hoped for earlier. He looks at the kids and they are already fast asleep. He smiles and begins to doze off.

Joey wakes up to the sun shining in the cave. He looks at both arms and does not see Pip or Nip. He starts to pace around nervously but then hears some laughter.

Joey: Pip! Nip! Where are you?

Nip: by the water.

Joey exits the cave and looks to the stream. The kids are by a rock just outside of the water. They are laughing.

Pip: We have a present for you.

Joey looks down at the rock and see's the biggest and fattest grub imaginable. Squirming slowly on the rock with a large green leaf on it. He looks at both Pip and Nip with a disgust look.

Joey: That's huge, are you guys going to eat that?

Pip and Nip: Nope, that's for you!

Joey looks at the grub and gags a little. He then remembers he told them he would eat a bug with them.

Joey: I'm going to eat that one?

Pip and Nip both smile and nod their little heads giggling. They then push the leaf over to Joey as if it were put on a silver platter. Joey shrugs his shoulders and throws the grub in the air. He catches it in his mouth and takes a little bite. It is the grossest thing he has ever tasted. He makes a dissatisfied face and spits it out. "Aw that was horrible," Joey quickly runs to the water to wash out the rest of the grub guts. The kids are hysterically laughing.

Joey: How can something be both crunchy and gooey at the same time.

He grabs some berries and swishes it in his mouth to remove the after taste. The kids are on the ground laughing.

Joey: Are you happy I tried it? I think I hate bugs. (He screams as he spits the taste out of his mouth).

Pip and Nip: Ha-ha, we are happy. We won't ask you again.

Joey: Ok, good. I am not a bug eating bird.

Pip: They taste great, and there are so many here.

Nip: Yeah, I love them too.

Joey smiles at them both and then looks around the oasis. This really is a good place for the family. They relax all day, playing in the water and foliage around them. It's past noon and Joey starts to worry about the parents. Are they ok? He figured they would be there about now. The kids don't seem to mind, Joey keeps these thoughts to himself. Still, he begins to worry. The day turns into night and still no sign of the parents. Joey realizes that they are not great climbers. Maybe it's just taking them a little longer. The kids snuggle next to Joey again in the small rock like cave. They fall asleep, but joey stays awake a while worrying about the parents.

The next morning Joey wakes up. The kids are still sleeping. Joey decides to fly up in the air and survey the area. Still no sign of Peter and Mary. He flies back down and greets the waking kids. The kids are less peppy this morning as they exit the cave.

Pip: Where's Mommy?

Nip: I miss mommy and daddy.

Joey: I'm sure they are just about to come back.

Joey surveyed for a few miles. He knows if they come at all, it will be later in the day. It's also much warmer than yesterday. They will probably be running out of water soon. After they all eat and drink some water; Joey tries to occupy their minds with something to avoid them thinking of their parents. What could they do though? Then a game hit's him, Target Practice! It always kept him occupied with his friends. The only issue, Pip and Nip cannot fly.

Joey then looks around. He sees some small rocks. He then looks at the top of the cave. They can go to the top of the cave and throw rocks at the target. What target would they throw at though? Joey then sees a good-sized stick and figures he will draw an outline of a car. Four squares representing the hood, windshield, the top of the car and the trunk. Then he explains the rules to the kids. They are excited to play. Joey flies them to the top of the cave and explains the point system. He then shows them how to play by throwing a rock, saying that he "never misses." Joey misses badly and the kids laugh.

Joey: Well, I usually play a little differently.

Pip and Nip: How do you play?

Joey then realizes he doesn't want to explain pooping on cars and changes the subject.

Joey: It was just different because it was on the beach. It takes practice.

Both kids throw the rocks and miss. Joey hands them another rock and then throws his. He hits the trunk. The boys miss again.

Pip: This is hard

Joey: It takes practice, one day you will be good at it; but only if you practice.

Nip: give me another one. I'll get it.

Nip throws the rock and hits the windshield square. Pip throws one and hits the back of trunk.

Joey: Wow now you guys are getting it. Having fun now?

Pip and Nip dance around the top of the rock with great pride. They are holding their hands and doing a little "Ring Around the Rousey" dance. Joey smiles, he has distracted them with a game he enjoyed as a child. The smile then turns to a worried look as he looks at the sun in the sky. It's the end of the day and the parents are still nowhere to be found. They keep playing the game into the evening, all three of them hitting more than they miss by the end. They are all showing improvement and even Joey is having some boyish fun.

Joey flies them down from the rock and they all have some laughs.

Nip: We are going to practice every day. When you come back, we will beat you!

Joey: You better practice if you are going to do that. (He chuckles)

Pip: Yeah, that's going to be fun to play every day.

Suddenly out of the bushes comes the parents. They are moving slowly, clearly exhausted from the trip.

Mary: My Babies!

Pip and Nip: Mom! Dad!

They all embrace each other, and Joey sits back with a sense of relief. It reminds him of his family at a joyous gathering.

Pip: Joey doesn't like bugs!

Nip: He also taught us a fun game.

Peter: Sounds like you all had some fun with Joey. Also, bugs are not for everyone.

Peter and Mary smile at Joey as if to say thank you. They look tired. Joey shows them the small rock like cave. They love it, shade for once. They eat and drink a little, they were all out of food and water. Bringing back an empty bottle each with some teeth marks from carrying it. Joey fills up the waters and picks some berries. He puts everything in the backpack, prepping for tomorrows travels. He wanted to give the family some alone time.

Peter meets him at the water and hugs him.

Peter: Thank you friend. We would of never have done it with the kids on our back. We barely made it on our own.

Joey: No problem, it was fun playing with the kids. I'll come back and see you when I fly down to visit my family.

Peter: Anytime Joe, anytime. We are headed to bed; promise you won't leave before saying goodbye. The kids have taken a liking to you.

Joey: I promise, Peter. I mean Pete.

Joey flies to the top on the cave and decides to think for a while. He throws a few rocks at the target just for fun. He thinks to himself, "I really want some salty fish. Tomorrow, I will head Northwest and make it to the beach. I can fish in the early morning the next day." He decides that's what he will do and slowly falls asleep.

Chapter Eleven: Batty Beach Fever

Joey wakes up and says goodbye to the family. They are all smiling and repeatedly tell him to come visit. He hugs each of them and then walks with Peter before he flies off. His backpack is stuffed with berries and water as he straps it on his back. Peter talks to Joey alone, just before he leaves.

Peter: Remember Joe, not everyone thinks like you do. People play dead in many ways. Some are not good souls like you are. You need to be careful of anyone's real intentions. That being said. If you find an animal that treats you, the way you have treated us. If they are a good soul. If they are looking for a place to live or need to crash for a few nights. You send them our way, regardless of the animal. That includes you as well.

Joey: Thanks Pete, I will do that.

Joey embraces Peter and soars through the air. He looks back to see the family looking up and waving. Joey meant what he said, this would be a place he would stop if he was ever in the area. Afterall, he is now Uncle Joey to the little ones.

Joey flies Northwest trying to cover more ground for Angle City, but also to get back to the beach for some familiar food. Who knows maybe he will meet some seagulls? He has not seen many on his trip and it would be comforting to see something or someone familiar.

Joey travels for hours; it is once again hot and dry. He flies fast while taking short breaks. He is out of protein and only has berries. Joey gobbles a small bunch of berries and washes it down with some water with every break he takes. He looks at the different sceneries and terrains as he travels, taking all the sights in.

The sun is covered with clouds late in the afternoon. This makes it very easy to travel faster. He arrives at the beach with a few hours of sunlight left. It's not a very populated beach. There are a few birds and other animals along the beachline. It's a little rocky and not a good place for a beach town, so there are only a few humans in the area. It's got some cliffs and greenery in several areas. Up at the top of the cliffs he sees two Seagulls. Joey perks up with giddy excitement. He flies up next to them and they give him a look as though he is not welcome.

Joey: He fellas! How's the fish swimming today.

The seagulls look at each other with disgust. "Do you know him, I don't?" One gull says.

The other one shakes his head and say "Nope!" They both then fly off and don't even acknowledging Joey was in the area.

Joey is set back and hurt, that someone would disregard him like that. That never happened at home. Perhaps it was because he had always known most of the animals in the area. When someone new came to the beach town, they usually were friendly. Maybe it was because they were the ones who were trying to fit in. This was the first time he thought back at what his parents and Tony had said to him, about things being different. He realized that not everyone would be friendly, and it was something he would have to expect at times. Afterall, if he was getting this in a beachy area with seagulls; he is sure to receive this kind of behavior in a city.

Joey sets his backpack down and begins to fish. The waves are choppy and not the best place to pinpoint fish. Not to mention he doesn't have trusty old Bob to give him the best fishing spots. He struggles a little bit, but in the end; he can snatches a few fish before sundown. It's windy and uncomfortable, he needs a place to settle down for the evening. He looks around and sees an elevated cave opening inside a cliff. It hangs over the beach in the middle of the rocky cliff. It's a place land animals or people would not be able to get to with ease. "That will do just perfect for tonight," he tells himself.

Joey enters the cave and goes about halfway in. He sits down and begins to eat a fish while watching the sun go down through the cave opening. The fish is delicious, the kind he really likes. He has another and then another.

Joey: MMM, this is so good. Joey, you caught yourself some good ones. (He says out loud with pride).

Suddenly Joey hears a voice and movement from the back of cave.

Voice: Who disturbs the owner of the cave!!!

Joey looks back and sees nothing, he looks side to side, and still nothing. He looks at the ground and sees a large pile of feces. Something has been living here, but what? He looks up and sees a dark figure with its wings spread wide. It frightens him. What should he do? In a panic he quickly thinks of what the possums do. Play dead!! Joey falls back and begins to play dead and closes his eyes, while sticking out his tongue. The creature then approaches him.

Voice: Hey buddy, what are you doing? (The voice changes to a different lighter pitched voice).

Joey: Playing dead.

Voice: Don't do that in a cave. That doesn't work.

Joey opens his eyes and sees a small bat. It looked bigger from a distance in the dark. He stands up and gives an embarrassed sigh as he brushes himself off.

Joey: Ugh, my names Joey.

Bert: My names Bert. I'm a bat, bats live in caves. You look like a seagull; seagulls don't live in caves.

Joey: I know, I'm traveling and just thought it would be a good place to rest for the night.

Bert: Ok, I'll let you stay on one condition. You let me eat some of whatever you were groaning about that tasted good. Deal?

Joey: Sure, it is fish. Do bats like fish?

Bert: I'm a Bat that lives alone in a cave, below my own poop. Do you think I am picky? (Bert says with some sarcasm)

Joey is shocked at the demeanor of the bat. He has the personality of a crotchety old man. Like his uncle and Bob, but less fun and cheeky. He seems smart but angry, not at Joey; but more at life itself. He takes a bite of the fish and gives a little satisfying mmm sound. Joey pulls out a bottle of water and offers it to Bert.

Joey: Water to wash it down?

Bert: Oh yes, there is no fresh water for miles.

Bert chugs the water down, he can barely hold the bottle. He then burps. He looks at Joey and says with a childish smirk.

Bert: That hit the spot. So young fellow, what brings you to this area?

Joey: I'm headed to Angle city.

Bert: Angle city, I've been there.

Joey perks up at Bert's response.

Joey: Really, what is it like?

Bert: It's a city.

Joey: Oh. (Joey is upset with the short response).

Bert: Why you going to the city? Seagulls are by the beach, mostly. They do not live in the city. Seagulls live by the beach, but not in caves. (Bert says jokingly)

Joey: I get it Bert, no caves. I just wanted to go somewhere different. See how I could fit in, see if I could help change the area for the better. Give myself some worldly knowledge and experience.

Bert: Aw to be young and motivated. I remember thinking like that. I've been many places and seen many things. You seem like a wise bird. Remember the wise can sometimes be looked at differently. The unwise are the ones who are sure of themselves, they do not see the progress of change. It is difficult to change the minds of many.

Joey: I know, but I just want to see what can be done. I come from a place where everyone works together. In my few days of traveling, I see that is not how the world is.

Bert: The world can be a selfish place. I have seen it. There is love though. It's important to find that love and stick to it. Without love, life is not worth living.

Joey is startled by the wise remarks. Bert went from being a grumpy old bat, to a wise old bat with words of wisdom. Clearly this bat has been around the block and Joey feels the need to pick his brain a little.

Joey: So how long have you been in this cave?

Bert: I don't know. A year, maybe two. It's all one long day. You are the first animal I have talked to in a long time. I used to travel the world seeking adventures and new experiences. Then I met a wonderful bat, and we had a child. Shortly after they passed away suddenly. Ever since then, I just kind of get by day by day.

Joey thinks of asking what happened, but he leaves the topic alone. He can only respond by saying, "I'm sorry." Bert then nods his head with sorrow and continues.

Bert: I've lived a long life, Joey. I've seen many joys and misfortunes, in many areas. A life without love is, is not a life worth living. I feel I have lived too long. Family is important, even if it's not your real family.

Joey sees the sadness in the old bat. It must be hard to be alone in a cave and not talk to anyone. He suddenly comes up with an idea. The Oasis! Peter did say that the Oasis would be a place he could send a friend. Joey brings up the idea to Bert.

Joey: Hey Bert, there is a place Southeast of here, way up in the mountains. It is about a day's travel. I just helped a family of possums get there. It has a cave, fresh water and all the bugs you can eat. It's a wonderful place, and the possums are a very good-natured family with two small children.

Bert: I don't know, maybe I'm too old to be with others. My outlook on life might not be the same with everything I've seen.

Joey: Nonsense Bert, it's always worth trying. A life without love is not worth living. You just said that. You must try.

Bert: Perhaps, it would be nice to have a cave and fresh water close together. I eat mostly mosquitos and there are more mosquitoes' around fresh water.

Joey: Yes, it really is an Oasis. So where is this other fresh water?

Bert: It's several miles Northeast of here. If you are going to Angle City, it would be on the way. I go there nightly for food and water. Never during the day, bats do not tan well.

Joey: Ok that is very helpful on my journey. But during the day for me.

Bert: Aw, the journey of life never ends until you do.

Joey smiles at all the bats little poetic sayings and jokes. Bert is a little socially awkward, but who wouldn't be when they are living alone in a cave. Joey then begins to ask about Angle City.

Joey: So, what is Angle City like; Bert?

Bert: Angle City is like most large cities. It is very fast paced, and every animal and human are always on the go.

Joey: Are there seagulls?

Bert: Not many, but I have seen some. Mostly pigeons, cockroaches, mice and rats. There was once a large seagull in the city many years ago. He talked like you do. He was young and was trying to change the world.

Joey: Really, what happened?

Bert: He was unsuccessful and eventually left. The bigger the population, the harder it is to instill change. I believe he realized that.

Joey: Well, I just want to see if I can make a difference. Contribute a little.

Bert: Aw, to be young. A good soul you are Joey. I wish the best for you.

Joey: Thank you Bert. Will you be going to the Oasis that I mentioned? (Joey yawns, it's been a long day).

Bert: Perhaps, I have not decided yet. Looks like you could use some sleep. I'm going to fly around for a while. Stay as long as you would like. I will see you in the morning if you are here. Thank you for my breakfast.

Joey retires for the night as the Bat flies off. He likes Bert. Joey figures he will stay and talk with him in the morning, before Bert goes to bed. It does not take

Joey long to fall asleep. While asleep he dreams of his family and when he was a young child. In the dream he is at the dinner table with his mother, father and Uncle. His mother is screaming at his uncle, but Joey cannot understand the words in the dream. Was this a dream or a flashback? Tony never came to dinner for as long as Joey could remember. All of the sudden, Joey can pick up a few words. Tony says to Joey's mom, "Don't worry, I will never go back; and we will never speak of this again."

Suddenly Joey wakes in a panic over the dream. Bert is standing next to him, watching him sleep.

Bert: Good Morning! You were dreaming. (Bert has a wide-eyed goofy smile on his face).

Joey: Aw, good morning. (He says startled by Bert).

Bert: I was thinking last night about the Oasis. I think I am going to give it a shot. The older I get, the easier I should make things on myself. Flying that much at night is getting to be too much.

Joey: I think you should. The possums are nice, and I think you would get along with them. Tell them Joey sent you!

Bert perks up with a sense of excitement. Joey can tell that he is both excited but also afraid. It is a similar feeling that Joey has felt on his journey. He understands the fear of the unknown. Perhaps it's something everyone feels at different points in someone's life. Joey feels the need to explain more.

Joey: Bert, the possum children. They both have a missing front leg, so they do not get around too well. The possums cannot fly. They could use someone like you to help them and teach them about the world.

Bert: Helping a family? That would make me feel useful at my age. OK, I think it's settled. I will go tonight.

Joey smiles and Bert nervously smiles back. He looks at Joey and feels the need to help him out in some way. Perhaps he can give him some advice.

Bert: Joey you really are a kind soul. I would like to give you some advice.

Joey: I'm all ears Bert. You've been around the block.

Bert talks of the warnings of trusting people, especially in the city and sings a poem.

Poem:

Not everyone you meet is honest.

Not everyone you meet is true.

But the ones that treat you right.

Always keep them close to you.

This world is full of crazy places.

Full of good, bad and funny faces.

And if you show the path of good intentions.

Others will follow you, even if there is tension.

Joey: Wow! (Joey is baffled at Bert) That was deep and surprisingly entertaining.

Bert: Thanks, I used to sing in the city.

Joey: I bet those possum kids would love to hear those poems.

Bert smiles at the thought. Then he looks at Joey sternly.

Bert: You need to get going. You need to stop hanging out with this old bat and continue your journey.

Joey: I know, thank you for the hospitality.

Bert: Remember Joey, most people do not have their minds made up on how to live, but some minds cannot be changed. Do not waste your time on the ones that cannot entertain two paths.

Joey: Thanks, Bert. The next time I see you, it will be at the Oasis.

Bert: Goodbye Joey.

Joey flies off and heads to the lake for water. While he flies, he thinks of some of the advice the old bat gave. He has concluded that not everyone is going to accept him and his ideas. Most beings will be standoffish to him at first.

Chapter Twelve: The Dock of the Bay

Joey continues to fly until he reaches the lake. He drinks some water and refills his bottles. The small lake is at the basin of the mountain. The lake looks to be low from the drought. Still no rain for weeks. Joey decides to go Northwest and fish again. He is now very close to the city. He has a water source, and hopefully a new great fishing spot. If he has those two things, all Joey will need to do is find shelter in the city. If Joey can find that, he can feel a sense of survival comfort.

The trip from the lake to the ocean is not too long. About an hour flying. Joey sees a bay, it's a large bay and very industrial. There are a few Seagulls around, and it reminds Joey of the bay from home. The only difference from this bay and Bro Beach, is there is much more going around it. It is very loud with construction and horns going off, but they still have a floating bait area like the one Bob hung out at. Joey heads over to the bait shop first. It's bigger than the one at home. It almost looks like there is a large home on the dock. Much different than the little shack that Joey is used to visiting. As Joey approaches, he sees a large sealion on the edge of the dock. She's very big, almost twice the size of Bob from home. Joey flies next to her to greet her. The Sealion looks perplexed at Joey as he lands next to her with a smile.

Joey: Hello, my name is Joey

The sealion sits up from the comfortable position and sighs. "Ugh my name is Shelby what do you want?"

Joey: I was wondering if you could point me in the direction of where the fish are today.

Shelby: Why would I do that, who are you? (Shelby is very confused by the friendliness of Joey).

Joey: I just came into the neighborhood and am looking to team up with others. If you show me where the fish are. I would love to give you a portion of the fish I catch. I would do this with a seal back home.

Shelby: That sounds interesting. I'll tell you what. There was some fish at the end of the dock this morning by the white boats. Try that area, I'm sure you'll have luck.

Joey: Thank you Shelby. Will you be here later in the day?

Shelby: I'm here every day catching some sunshine during the day.

Joey: Great, maybe this can be our little thing.

Shelby: I doubt you'll come back with fish for me.

Joey: Have a little faith in others Shelby.

Shelby: I need to see the action before I instill faith in you Joey. If you come back, we will talk more. You have until sundown.

Joey: You will not be disappointed. (Joey says with excitement and then flies off).

Shelby looks with confusion at Joey as he flies off. Joey is all hyped up with excitement. Could he establish a relationship with this sealion? This area is very close to the city. This could be an ongoing relationship, like his uncle and Bob had. He reaches the end of the dock with a few white boats that are docked up. The boats don't seem to be used much and there are some kelp paddies everywhere. This is a great spot for fish to swim.

Joey takes off his backpack and finds a bucket on one of the boats. He places the bucket and red backpack on the top of one of the larger boats. Flying up in the air, he looks down and sees the fish. Joey catches the fish and places them in the bucket. The bucket fills quickly. He then goes back to fill what room he has in his backpack. As Joey circles around, he catches in the corner of his eye, another seagull grabbing his bucket full of fish. The seagull then flies off. "Hey you! Stop!" Joey says with anger.

Joey flies as fast as he can after the seagull. Angerly he repeatedly shouts "Wait!" and "Stop!" as he gains ground. They fly over the docks and by the beach area. Joey gains and gains on the seagull. Finally, he tackles the bird in the air and they both land in the sand on the beach. Both are lying in aching pains, with the bucket of fish tipped over in the middle of them. Joey pops up then grabs the bucket and picks up the fish that fell out along the sand. He then brushes himself off, he is covered in sand from head to toe. Joey yells out in frustration, "Ugh, so sandy."

The other seagull sits up from the fall and then addresses Joey with a perplexed expression and says, "How do you know my name?"

Joey brushes off the rest of the sand and looks at the seagull. It's a female most likely close to his age. "Your name is Sandy?"

Sandy: Yes Sandy, like the sand on the beach.

Joey: Hello Sandy, my name is Joey. Why did you grab my bucket? (He says angerly)

Sandy: I saw it had fish in it. I was watching you from a distance. You catch fish well. I wish I could catch fish like that.

Joey: But why would you steal it from me.

Sandy: Because I'm hungry and need to eat. I do not catch fish well; I usually grab what I can from boats and scavenge.

Joey: Well, why wouldn't you just ask? I would have given you one.

Sandy: You would just give it to me? (She says with another perplexed expression).

Joey: Yes, I would just give it to you. You do not just steal things. It's not right.

Sandy: I always just take what I need. I've never known any other way.

Joey: You never share?

Sandy: No, I have always been on my own.

Joey: I don't believe that. What about your parents.

Sandy: I don't remember them. I've been on my own since I was little.

Joey subdues his anger a little after hearing Sandy does not have anyone in her life. He empathizes a little with her situation and changes his tone to a nicer one.

Joey: Listen Sandy, I need to give a few of these fish to the sealion who helped me find the spot. However, I will give you one fish.

Joey pulls out the biggest fish in the bucket and hands it to Sandy. She instantly devours the fish and burps.

Sandy: Aww, that was so tasty. If only I had fresh water.

Joey sighs a little and then tells Sandy to follow him back to the boat where his backpack is. He's flustered at Sandy's outlook on life. How she just thinks for herself. They start flying back to the boat. When they arrive, he takes out a water bottle. Sandy immediately gulps the water down. She was obviously both very hungry and thirsty. Joey watches in amazement at how fast she drinks the bottle. Then for the first time Sandy flashes a smile at Joey and says, "Thank you." Joey cannot help but smile back and says, "you are welcome." There is an awkward silence until Joey decides to break it with a standard mundane question.

Joey: So where do you live?

Sandy: I don't know, I guess I live right here.

Joey: No, I mean where do you go to sleep.

Sandy: Wherever I want to, usually around here somewhere.

Joey: So, you don't have a permanent place? You are just a nomad?

Sandy: Pretty much. Why, where do you live?

Suddenly Joey stops and thinks to himself. He also does not have an answer to that question. He comes up with the best answer he can think of.

Joey: I'm moving to the city.

Sandy: The city? what's in the city?

Joey: Um, I'm not sure. I haven't been there yet.

Sandy: I guess we are both nomads. (She says with a sarcastic smirk).

Joey: Yeah, I guess we are.

Sandy: Where do you get water? It's been so dry lately.

Joey: There is a lake Southeast of here. It's not too far.

Sandy: Southeast?

Joey realizes that Sandy does not know how to navigate like some of the other animals he has met on his journey. She seems to lack in some basic survival skills. How she has survived this long is beyond Joey. Joey reluctantly teaches her, the skills of navigating the sun. She sort of gets it, but not entirely and the time goes by.

Then Joey looks at the sun. It's starting to set, and he needs to get the fish to Shelby. He tells Sandy to wait there and rushes to the dock with the bucket. There he sees Shelby.

Joey: Shelby! I told you I'd come back.

Shelby: Lord heaven! you are a bird of your word!

Shelby grabs the three fish Joey throws to her while still flying and gulps one down.

Joey: Shelby am I trustworthy?

Shelby: You sure are, Joey.

Joey: OK, I'll be coming by for forecasts in the future. Same Deal?

Shelby: Same Deal! Have a good night!

Joey rushes back to the boats. He just realized he left his red backpack with

Sandy. He doesn't think that she will run off with it, but he just doesn't know for sure. Afterall, she did try to steal the bucket. Joey flies back and see's Sandy sitting by the boat like they were before, the red backpack has not been touched. She hasn't moved from her spot. Joey flies next to her and addresses her, this time with a softer tone.

Joey: You didn't leave or take the backpack?

Sandy: You told me to wait. I figured you were coming back.

Suddenly, Joey had a newfound respect for Sandy. She wasn't bad, she was just doing what she needed to do to survive. If he was in her situation, he most likely would have done the same thing. Joey decides he is going to help her.

Joey: Listen Sandy, I would like to show you where the lake is tomorrow. Then we can come back to the bay, and I will also show you how to fish. This way you do not have to steal from others. How does that sound?

Sandy: You would do that for me? (Sandy says intuitively with a sense of surprise).

Joey: Sure, I think knowing how to survive is very important. Also, it will keep you from stealing my fish. (Joey says jokingly with a smile).

Sandy: Ok, but it might take me a while.

Joey: That's ok, it will be a lesson for both of us. We will start tomorrow in the morning.

Sandy: Ok, but on one condition, we eat more fish now. (She says with grin).

The sun starts to set, and Joey and Sandy eat some fish and drink some water. They both retire to a different boat and begin to fall asleep. As the day turns to night Sandy addresses Joey one last time.

Sandy: Hey Joey?

Joey: What Sandy?

Sandy: Thank you!

Joey smiles at the appreciation as he closes his eyes. It feels good knowing he is helping someone out. It's also nice to see another Seagull and have some company.

Chapter Thirteen: The Student Teacher

The next morning Sandy wakes up Joey at the first sign of light. It's very clear that she is excited to learn some new skills. They each eat a fish and drink the remaining water they have. "Don't worry, we will have more fish and water when we get back," Joey assures Sandy.

They fly off into the day and Joey begins teaching Sandy navigation of the sun, as well as the importance of food, shelter and water. Sandy is slow at first and asks a few questions as they go, but she starts to pick it up. Like the family of possums, Joey feels a sense of pride teaching what he knows to someone else. His father and uncle taught him well. To teach it and help someone else in need, feels like the right thing to do.

They get to the basin of the lake and Joey explains drinking a lot of water to fill up, so they do not run out right away. Sandy drinks as much as she can possibly drink and then burps. "I guess I was thirsty," she says with an embarrassed smile.

After filling up the water bottles, they spend a little time looking at the mountains in the distance. Sandy has never been this far east before and loves it. They start to head back, and Joey again explains the importance of Navigation. Sandy is now picking it up and starts to navigate herself, this time with Joey following. Her demeanor has gone from defensive when they first met, to now full of excitement and wonder. She had spent most of her life on her own doing just what she could to survive. With these new learned skills, she feels she can now take control of a new destiny; whatever that happens to be.

They arrive back at the docks and begin to fish. Joey teachers her his circle technique. Circling around the area and spotting a fish. Then dive down and grab the fish with your mouth, and then bring the fish back to the bucket. Sandy struggles for the first few hours. She doesn't catch a single fish, and Joey has caught about a dozen. She clearly is getting very frustrated and takes a break on the dock.

Sandy: I'll never get it; I might as well quit!

Joey: You can't quit! It takes time. When I was younger it took me hundreds of times. You'll get it, you just need to keep working at it.

Sandy: That's easy for you to say. Look, you get one almost every time! (She points to the bucket)

Joey: I know, but I have been doing this for many years. No one is an expert at something when they first start. Just keep working at it!

Sandy: Fine, I'll try again!

She starts to get better at circling and finding the fish, but she continues to fail at grabbing the fish. She gets the fish, but the fish keeps squirming out of her mouth as she flies back up. As the day goes on, she still has not caught anything. She flies to the dock again. This time very angry.

Sandy: Ugh, I just, I just can't!

Joey takes his wing and puts it on her shoulder. He looks at her with a smile and she looks at him with a frustrated face. He then says softly to her, "Think of it as a game and don't take it so seriously." Sandy chuckles then looks at the water. She takes a deep sigh and flies back up in the air. She circles around three times and squints at the target. It's a good-sized fish. She swoops down and grabs the fish; it wiggles as hard as it can and slips out of her mouth as she goes up in the air. This time she catches it before it falls. She's got it! She quickly heads back to the dock where the bucket is. She is clearly very excited for herself and has a smile going from ear to ear, along with the fish in her mouth. She spits the fish in the bucket and then screams.

Sandy: I got one! I got one!

Sandy then does a little strutting dance, then a moonwalk that makes Joey laugh.

Joey: Great Job! See I told you that you could do it. It just takes time.

Sandy: Yeah, I guess I can (She says with a smile).

Joey: You can do anything if you work hard at it. It looks like our bucket is full, but we still have one last thing to do.

Sandy: What's that?

Joey: There is a sealion that has helped us find the fish. We need to say thank you to her by giving her a few fish that we caught.

Sandy is a little put off by the notion of sharing with someone who did not catch the fish.

Sandy: Why, she didn't catch the fish. She didn't put in the work.

Joey: I know, but she helped us find the fishing spot yesterday. If we show good faith to her, she will continue to find us more fishing spots.

Sandy: Oh, I guess that sounds fair (she says this reluctantly but accepting of the idea).

Joey: Yes, I would also like for you to give it to her. So, she knows who you are.

Sandy: Ok, let's get this over with (she says like a disappointed child).

Joey grabs the bucket and they both fly to see Shelby. He greets Shelby and then introduces Shelby to Sandy. They both fly onto the dock.

Joey: Hey Shelby, this is Sandy.

Shelby: Hello there Sandy.

Sandy: Hi Shelby, nice to meet you. Um, we have something for you.

Sandy grabs two fish from the bucket and places them next to Shelby. Then smiles at Shelby in a shy manor.

Shelby: Oh, bless you child! If you come by tomorrow, I will continue to give you updates on the fish. The same deal I have with Joey.

Sandy: Thank you Shelby! It was a pleasure meeting you. Any friend of Joey is a friend of mine.

Shelby: I like her Joey; you pick your friends well.

Joey: Aw thanks Shelby. (he says a little embarrassed).

They head back to the dock and eat a few fish to celebrate the long day. Sandy stops eating for a second and asks Joey a few questions.

Sandy: So, Joey? Why would we give our hard-earned fish to Shelby, when we were the ones who caught them?

Joey: Because she can help us find the fish when they move. She is part of the team. We can get more done together, than if we try alone. It's easier to survive when we work together. If we spent time looking for fishing spots, we wouldn't have time to fish.

Sandy: I guess you are right; I've never really worked as a team. It does feel good knowing you are working towards a bigger goal.

Joey: Exactly! When we all strive for the same thing. We all win.

Sandy yawns and can barely keep her eyes open. It's been a long day. They both retire to each other's boat, the same as last night. It was a long day. Joey sits awake and decides he is going to help Sandy a little more before he visits the city. This was not his plan, but he wants to help her out and make sure she can survive an honest way. It's also nice to have a fishing partner again.

The next few weeks are very similar. Every other day or so, they take a trip to the lake for fresh water. Sandy can now navigate her way back and forth to the lake. Then they fish for a bit and meet up with Shelby. Shelby tells them about the hot spots for catching fish. They were able to find a few extra buckets and a few extra empty water bottles. They now have a great survival system, and everything is great.

Joey still knows he wants to go to the city, and he is not sure how Sandy will take it. This would not be goodbye. Afterall, he still will need to fish. He just knows things are going well, and he doesn't want to disappoint her. He decides to address it one day after fishing.

Joey decides to surprise her with something before breaking the news, but with what? He roams the bay looking through boats. What could he possibly give to her? After about an hour he sees a big yacht on the edge of a dock. It's on the other side of the bay from where they stay. There is a bunch of children's toys, the owner must have kids. In the corner he sees the perfect gift. It's a small yellow backpack. Sandy had commented several times on his red backpack, and how it was a gift his mother gave it to him. What a perfect gift!

Joey grabs the backpack and heads back. Sandy is fishing and doing very well. He takes a long roundabout way to avoid Sandy seeing him. He wants it to be a surprise. He flies all around her from a distance and enters the dock from the land side. All of the sudden, Sandy sees Joey and smiles. She yells out, "Joey!"

Joey doesn't acknowledge her and quickly runs to his boat. Sandy begins to fly in and Joey yells, "Hold on!" He quickly runs inside the boat and hides the backpack under the seat. Sandy lands on the dock and starts calling out to Joey with a sense of confusion and concern.

Sandy: Joey? What are you doing?

Joey: Nothing.

Sandy: Oh, you look like you were hiding something.

Joey: No, I just, I just needed to go to the bathroom. (It was the first excuse he could come up with).

Sandy: Um, Ok. Is everything OK? (She asks with a sense of concern).

Joey decides this is the time to let her know he is going to check out the city. He hesitates for a few seconds and begins to speak.

Joey: Listen Sandy, I have decided that I will be headed to the city for a day or two. I will be back though. I just need to experience the city in full.

Sandy: I knew you were going to say that eventually. What should I do? (She asks with some self-doubt).

Joey: I think you should continue fishing and getting water. We have a good thing going, and I will be back. I just need to check the city out. It was always the plan.

Sandy: I know, I just finally got used to being around someone else. It feels good to not always be alone.

Joey: And you won't! I have decided this will be where I hang my hat most of the time. I just need to do this. (Joey says with affirmation).

Sandy: Will I need to do something different when you are not here?

Joey: No, you know what you are doing now. Visit Shelby, fish and always make sure you have enough water.

Sandy: How will I carry the water bottles back?

Joey smiles at the questions. Then he heads back into the boat and grabs the small yellow backpack. He exits the boat with a grin, showing the backpack off. Sandy puts her wings to her mouth in surprise.

Sandy: For me?

Joey: Now we both have one.

Sandy: No one has ever gotten me a present before. (She hugs Joey).

Joey: Yeah, Well I wanted to make sure you had everything you needed.

Sandy: I do, you are coming back though, right?

Joey: Yes, of course. We got a good thing going here. Now how did you do fishing today?

Sandy: Check this out! (she says with excitement).

Sandy shows her the buckets full of fish. They are overflowing out of the bucket. Joey has taught her well, and these results further confirm that she can handle the days he is gone on her own. He smiles with pride not only for her, but for himself. He knows he has taught her a skill she can use for the rest of her life. They both fly to Shelby and give her a few fish. After that, they fly back to the dock and have themselves some fish. They laugh reminiscing over the struggles she had in the beginning, then they retire to each other's boat.

There is a creature by the end of the dock watching them as they settle in for the evening. He was watching for a while. It was Speedy. Speedy smiles and says to himself, "He is still doing ok." Then he runs off fast, as he always does, back to the beach city.

As Joey begins to nod off into the night, he hears a close thumping sound. He awakes startled and says softly, "Who's there?" It's Sandy. Without a word she crawls next to Joey and puts her head to his shoulder. She then places her wing across his chest and closes her eyes. Joey smiles, and then closes his eyes. Not a word is spoken, they both blissfully fall asleep.

Chapter Fourteen: The Big City

Joey wakes up with a stretch and a yawn. He looks over to Sandy, and she is still sleeping. She looks so blissfully beautiful as light begins to shine on the boat. He doesn't want to wake her. He slips away from her arm and begins to pack for his trip. He looks at her one last time and smiles. Then he places a fish next to her, a surprise for when she wakes up. Then he pauses for a second, takes a deep breath and flies off into the sky. He is headed for the city.

Joey flies through air and looks at the terrain of the earth. It begins to get flatter and more densely populated. The beauty of the beach and mountains are now nonexistent. It's buildings and streets everywhere, the tall buildings keep getting larger. He continues to fly into the city. The peaceful serenity is replaced with the noises of people and cars. The air is not as clean and there are few water sources. This is not what Joey is used to.

Joey enters the heart of the city and lands on the street. It's crowded with people. He walks around looking up at all the signs and buildings. The distraction keeps him from knowing his surroundings. People keep almost kicking him from walking. They are walking in all different directions. Joey starts to feel some anxiety and begins looking in all different directions. Suddenly, he gets kicked by a large boot. It sends him back on his bottom. He is dazed and confused about what's going around him. Then he is kicked again by a jogger. "Damn bird!" a voice screams out.

Joey manages to place his wings on the ground. He pushes himself up and looks around. He needs to rest, but where? Suddenly a voice is heard, "Hey, Hey Seagull, up here!" Joey looks up and sees a pigeon waving his arms.

"Up here, It's safer! Dodge left, dodge right and come up here!"

Joey dodges a few people and then, with all his strength; he flies off to the corner of an elevated parking lot. He lands next to the Pigeon. Joey is breathing heavily. He is both exhausted and recovering from a panic. He addresses the pigeon who guided him.

Joey: Wow, thanks. That was intense. People do not watch where they are going around here!

Pigeon: Yeah, you really can't go down to the ground during high foot traffic times. You'll get yourself killed in the city like that.

Joey: Wish I knew that ten minutes ago. (He says as he finally calms down a bit) My name is Joey.

Pigeon: The name's Larry. Those two right there are Joyce and Kevin.

Joey looks at the other pigeons, he didn't even recognize them in the state of panic he was in. He then looks around and sees dozens of other pigeons just hanging out at the top of the empty rooftop parking lot. The lower levels look to be abandoned and boarded up. The pigeons are all scattered around in no order. Larry looks to be the elder pigeon. They all look dirty with rugged feathers. He addresses the three of them.

Joey: Hey Everyone. I just came into the city for the first time. Is it always that chaotic? (Joey says with frustration).

Larry: That's nothing, you should see it at the beginning and end of each day. So, what are you doing here? We do not see many seagulls in this area anymore.

Joey: Well, I just wanted to come to the city and check it out.

Joyce: Why?

Kevin: Yeah, why?

Larry: Yeah, I'm going to have to side with these two on this, and ask why? This area stinks.

Joey: I just wanted to see how things were done in the area. You know- how the city works together.

Joyce: Work together, no we do not do that here.

Kevin: Yeah, there is no working together around here.

Joey: How do you all survive.

Larry: We just take what we can get from the ground. When we can.

Joey: What do you do for water?

Joyce: There's a fountain in the heart of the city. We go there when it is not overcrowded with people and sip from it.

Joey: You all don't save food and water for later?

Larry: No, if we did save it; others would come and take it. We just scavenge. This is the city young fellow.

Joey looks around at the parking garage. It's full of birds, all looking like they struggle. The parking lot is covered in bird poop and trash. It looks like a horrible place to live. The lower levels are boarded and caged up with a few holes for birds to fly in and out of. There are two penthouses on the top at each side. A few falcons are on them, all separated from each other; they are clearly not working together. It's clear they have no system of survival, and they are in survival mode.

Joey: So, what do you guys do every day?

Kevin: We do what we can to survive kid. (He says in a sarcastic way) It's all we can do.

Joey: Wouldn't it be easier to work together?

Larry: Hey, this kid doesn't get it. (Larry addresses the other two pigeons, then looks at Joey and says slowly) This here is the city, Joey.

Joey: No, I get it. However, if you all work together. You could survive better, together.

The pigeons start to laugh and talk to themselves. They are starting to lose interest in Joey and his radical talking. Joey is losing them. Then he gets an idea. The game Target Practice! It worked with the possum kids, it worked with his friends. Maybe it could work here. Joey interrupts the pigeons talking softly to themselves and asks if they want to play a game.

Joey: Hey guys, how would you like to play a game? It involves pooping on nice cars.

The pigeons listen to Joey with a smile as he tries to explain the game. Kevin interrupts Joey.

Kevin: Oh, we have played something like this. We call it Bombs Away!

Joey: Bombs Away?

Joyce: Hey everyone, we are playing Bombs Away! Who wants to play! (She screams at the rooftop so all the other pigeons can hear them).

Suddenly almost all the pigeons start flying over with big smiles. They are all giddy with excitement. Voices are heard by Joey saying things like "This will be fun," and "It's been a while." Joyce looks at Joey and says with a mysterious grin, "Follow us."

All the birds fly onto a nearby light pole. They line up, one by one above the street corner. Joey joins them. The pigeons are all giggling like little school children. "Now remember everyone, when we yell Bombs Away, let one out!" Larry says to all the pigeons. Joey assumes that means poop off the light pole.

Suddenly a blue Prius drives by and sits at the traffic light right under the birds. "BOMBS AWAY!" a few of them yell. Everyone lets one out and the car is instantly covered in excrement. The once blue Prius is now covered in white. The windshield is no longer visible.

The window rolls down and yells, "Are you kidding me!"

Then another, "BOMBS AWAY!" The car is again covered, and the pigeons fly back to the parking lot structure. They are all laughing uncontrollably, some pigeons are on their backs rolling with laughter, like a hyena. Once Joey catches his breath from laughing, he addresses the pigeons.

Joey: That's a little different from the game I play, but I have to say; it's just as fun.

Kevin: An oldie, but goodie. I guess all birds have a passion for pooping on cars.

Larry: Yeah, that made me feel young again!

Joyce: We all got that car good!

Joey pauses for a second and thinks to himself. In some strange way, that was an example of great teamwork. He addresses all the pigeons.

Joey: Hey everyone, now how long would it take for just one bird to dirty that car like we did?

Kevin: Unless I found a burrito on the side of the road, it would take weeks. Believe me, I've tried. (He says jokingly).

Joey: Exactly, we accomplished something that would have been nearly impossible by ourselves. Instead, we did it together in a just a few seconds. Imagine if you applied this teamwork to everyday life and survival.

Larry nods at Joey. He knows the point he is now trying to make. He wants the rest of the pigeons to hear him out.

Larry: Go on Joey, we would like to hear more. You have our attention.

Joey: If we all worked together, we could accomplish so much more than if we work alone. It sounds complicated, but once everyone contributes it becomes easier for all of us.

The pigeons mutter to themselves, agreeing to what has been said. A voice in the crowd yells "this guy makes sense, tell us more!"

Joey begins explaining the importance of water, food and shelter. He talks of the town he grew up in, the system that his father made for the beach town. The pigeons are all ears. He speaks of getting water with bottles, birds catching fish and others cleaning up the areas for others to live. He talks about gathering materials from the human trash cans for shelter and the distributing of food. It is all well received, and pigeons get excited by the new ideas. The crowd disperses for the evening, they are all talking about the new ideas for a better future. Kevin and Joyce smile at Joey with approval, nod and then walk away. Larry stays back to talk with Joey.

Larry: This all sounds great Joey, I'm sure the falcons would love to help. We have an issue when it comes to going through trash.

Joey: What's the issue? In this large city; I'm sure there is a wealth of food and materials in the trash.

Larry: There is Joey, but the Rats control the trash. They do not like it when other animals go through the trash. They fight back. They live at the bottom level. Other animals in the middle levels would probably agree, but not the rats.

Joey: Well maybe, we can reason with them?

Larry: Others have tried, it doesn't work.

Joey: Well, we must try Larry. It's worth trying! (He says convincingly)

Larry smiles at Joey. He sighs and addresses Joey with more respect than he has before.

Larry: I was young like you once, maybe you're right. Maybe it is time for a change. This time it could be different.

Joey: This time? You mean it was tried before?

Larry: Yes, a few animals tried this before many years ago. It worked for a while. We saw improvement, but in the end it didn't work. You can stay on the roof tonight with us, but please do me a favor. Will you fly around the city at night? Take in the sites, you'll understand what you are dealing with.

Joey: I will, Larry. It can work, I know it can.

Larry: Well, talk tomorrow, if you still think that; then we will give it a try.

Larry walks away and Joey looks at the city. The sunlight is fading, and the lights of the city are showing up. He takes a second and the flies off going from block to block checking out the city. The lights are bright and there are people at every corner. It's still very loud. He flies through some alleyways and sees some homeless humans. They look almost as bad as some of the animals. As he takes breaks, he lands on a few rooftops. He sees a few dead birds and is disgusted at the rotting corpses. He cannot even tell what kind of bird it is. He hears people arguing in the streets and honking of horns. The nightlife looks to be angry and dangerous. Does this go on all night, he asks himself? This is not a peaceful place to sleep.

Joey flies back to the elevated parking structure. He is in a state of shock of the city conditions. He takes a corner of the rooftop parking lot to sleep. It's not near anyone else. He then rests his head on his backpack that is still full of fish. He didn't eat this morning, there was too much going on; he forgot. He thinks of how he can help, is it even possible. He is going to try, he must. The sound of sirens and traffic fill the air of the night. He tosses and turns throughout the night from the noises around him, and the noises in his own head.

Chapter Fifteen: The Plan

Joey wakes up to the sun shining on his face. It was a restless night, and his mind was racing all night with what to do next. Larry is on the edge of the parapet looking down at the city. It looks as though he is also in deep thought. Joey groggily addresses Larry.

Joey: Good Morning, Larry.

Larry: Tough night sleeping?

Joey: Yeah, the noise. It never stops.

Larry: You get used to it. I was thinking last night, Joey. Something must change.

Joey: I was thinking too, it can be done. This won't come easy though.

Larry looks at Joey, he sighs and then nods. He then looks up at the penthouse and then addresses Joey.

Larry: I'd like to introduce you to Freddy. He is an older Falcon that sits on top of the penthouse of the parking lot. He's been here a long time. If there is someone who can help get the falcons and other animals to join us. It would be him.

Joey: That's great, we will need larger birds for transporting water and fishing.

Larry: Would you be able to tell him a plan?

Joey: A Plan? Can you give me an hour?

Larry: Sure, I'll come back shortly. Hey Joey!

Joey: Yes, Larry?

Larry: Keep the plan simple. Don't overwhelm everyone.

Larry nods at Joey and then flies off to the penthouse. Joey starts to think of how his father ran the beach, and all the advice he gave them. He looks around the parking lot and finds a piece of plywood and a rusty nail. He decides to write out the plan.

Large birds transport water in bottles and fish for food.

Pigeons / Rats scavenge food and items from the ground and trash

Smaller animals clean the parking lot and help with shelter

Birds of all kinds can transport food and water to others

Fast animals can provide communication on how things are going throughout the city

All animals are welcomed and can join if they desire

Joey does simple drawings of the animals and items. Then he puts arrows showing what and where they are going. Then at the end, he shows a few pictures of different animals with smiley faces on them. Showing all that participate are welcomed into the community system. Joey feels this best simplifies what he is trying to say. There is more to it, but for a sales pitch with a time constraint; this will have to do.

Larry flies over, just as Joey is finishing up. Joey shows him the plywood. Larry smiles and says with a chuckle, "honestly, not bad. That is very creative." They both fly over to the falcons. It's just Freddy on the penthouse now, the other birds are gone for the moment.

Larry: Hi Freddy, I'd like you to meet Joey. He has some ideas on how to make things better.

Freddy: Hello Joey, what ideas do you have?

Joey shows Freddy the piece of plywood and explains everything in detail. He explains how if they all work together, survival will be easier. Freddy nods at the idea and addresses Joey.

Freddy: This looks like a great idea. Very similar to something we have heard in the past. I'm sure I could get the other falcons and even the crows to agree on this. There one issue though, we do not know how to fish. I'm not sure if we even like fish?

Joey takes off his backpack and takes out three fish. He has been so busy that he forgot to eat again, and his stomach is growling.

Joey: I have some here. Let's all have one.

They all sit back and eat some fish. Both Larry and Freddy are blown away at the food they have ate. They never tasted something so good.

Freddy: Wow, this is amazing. We could eat this all day.

Larry: Yes, I didn't expect this. It is so succulent.

Joey: You know, I could teach you all how to fish? If the other birds were willing?

Freddy: Well, if they could taste this fish. I'm sure they would want to learn.

Joey takes out the rest of his fish and lays it on the penthouse. He then addresses Freddy and gives a proposition.

Joey: How's this? You give the birds some fish and let them taste it. I will come back tomorrow, and if the other birds want to learn how to fish, we can teach them.

Freddy: We?

Joey: There is another Seagull, her name is Sandy. She is probably fishing right now. We can teach you.

Freddy: Ok, young fellow. Let me talk to the other birds. If they are on board. We will give it a shot. Would you leave the board with commandments, so I can explain it to others?

Joey: Sure thing, I'll be back tomorrow afternoon.

Joey says farewell to both and then flies off back to the bay. He wants to check on Sandy and maybe fish a little. As he flies, he thinks of all the different ways this plan could work. He also thinks of how it could backfire. It's sure going to take a lot of effort to put this whole thing together.

Joey flies back to the bay with some sunlight left. He gets to the dock and does not see Sandy. He looks down at the edge of the dock and sees a bunch of buckets full of fish. Sandy has been doing well, but where is she? Did she go get water? Suddenly Sandy flies in behind him, holding another full bucket of fish.

Sandy: Joey! (She hugs Joey).

Joey: Hey Sandy! Wow you are really getting good at fishing. Where were you?

Sandy: Shelby changed the fishing spot. It's a very good one. You were right about keeping Shelby on the team.

Joey: That's great! Hey, I must ask you something. You are getting so good at fishing; would you be able to help me teach other birds to fish? For the city, so we can all work together.

Sandy looks at Joey and gives a delighted look. She is flattered that Joey would ask her to help.

Sandy: Sure, so the trip went well?

Joey: Yeah, we could have something going. Nothing set in stone yet, just on plywood. I think we could make the area better.

Sandy: I'm happy to help, I like what you have done so far for me and Shelby. If everyone could work together, it makes things easier. Just like you said. You look tired?

Joey: I am, the city was a lot.

Sandy: Yeah, I used to go there from time to time. It was a hard place to survive. I'd be happy to help in any way I can.

Joey: Thanks Sandy, I need your help on this.

Sandy smiles and gives Joey another hug.

Sandy: You look tired, lay down.

Joey lies down and sandy brings over some fish. They eat the fish and drink some water. Then Sandy lies next to him.

Sandy: Do you think we can get everyone to work together?

Joey: I don't know. We are going to try though.

Joey falls asleep almost immediately. It's comforting to not be in the city. The bay is much quieter at night. It's also great to have Sandy next to him. There is a comfort to life when she is around him. He realizes that he is beginning to have strong feelings for her.

Chapter Sixteen: The Reform

Joey wakes the next morning to the sun already up. He looks next to him and sees Sandy is not there. He looks out to the dock and Sandy is packing his backpack full of fish and waters. She looks at him and smiles. "You were tired, you were snoring all night," she giggles. She helps him with the backpack and says, "I'll see you later today, hopefully with some other birds." Joey smiles and begins to take off. Suddenly, Sandy grabs his shoulder and twists him around. She gives him a big kiss. "For good luck," she says. They both bashfully smile at each other and then he flies off.

The kiss puts Joey in a good mood as he flies into the heart of the city. When he arrives to the city he sees something extraordinary. All the birds have cleaned the top of the rooftop. They are working together. The falcons, pigeons and crows are all sweeping and cleaning with items they found in the city. As Joey flies in, he sees something else. Above one of the Penthouses is the plywood. The plywood with the writings and drawings he had made the day before. They hung it up. So, everyone could read it.

Joey flies onto the rooftop and is greeted by Larry. Joey has a confused look on his face.

Joey: What is everyone doing?

Larry: They are cleaning the rooftop. We are getting ready to make this a home. Under your guidance. We will build little shelters for everyone.

Joey: Everyone wants to participate?

Larry: Yes, Freddy told some of the other birds. Then word of mouth came around. Once they saw the plywood hung up. They all bought in.

Joey: Who hung up the plywood?

Larry: Freddy did.

Joey looks up at the penthouse and sees Freddy. Freddy stares back, nods to Joey and then turns away.

Joey: Where did they get all the materials for cleaning?

Larry: They gathered materials from the trash.

Joey: The trash? What about the rats? Are they on board?

Larry: We haven't talked to the Rats yet. We were hoping you would talk to them. It won't be easy.

Joey: Yeah, I can do that.

Larry: Sounds good, first I would like you to address everyone.

Larry goes to the middle of the parking lot rooftop. Then he yells very loudly so everyone can hear them.

Larry: Hey everyone! Stop what you are doing! Joey has something to say to everyone.

All the birds fly over and gather around Joey. Freddy flies next to Joey. The looks on all their faces are determined. They look as though they are going to hang on every word that Joey says. Joey looks around at all of them. He knows he has to say something that brings motivation.

Joey: Um, Hey everyone.

Everyone is quiet. Still looking for guidance. Joey is nervous.

Joey: So, first off great job! I can barely recognize this rooftop from before. As we finish cleaning, we need to address three main things. These three main things are food, water and shelter. I'd like us to start making nesting huts for each animal. We can use the rooftop, penthouse and the floor below us. I'd also like to construct a team that will be responsible for food and water.

Freddy: I've already set up the team Joey.

Freddy points to some falcons and crows. They have a scary look on their face, of determination.

Joey: Ok, they look like they will do. Do any of you know how to fish?

The birds look at each other and shake their heads no. Still with grimaces on their faces.

Joey: Ok, I want to take you to the bay. I have someone who can teach you. We should do this now. In the meantime, everyone please continue to clean and gather materials. We need to start building shelters for everyone.

Larry: What about the rats?

Joey: I can talk to them when I get back. In the meantime, here is some fish and water for everyone.

Joey empties his backpack and dumps all the fish and water bottles onto the rooftop. The birds begin to eat the fish and drink the water. Passing it around in circles so everyone gets a fair share. Joey turns to Larry and Freddy.

Joey: I'm going to take this team to the bay. I have someone who can teach them what is needed. This will keep us all filled with water and food.

Larry: Ok, but again, what about the rats?

Joey: Let's get the basics down. I'll be back later today to talk to the rats.

Larry: Ok Joey.

Freddy: Larry's right about the rats. It will need to be addressed, but this sounds like a great game plan.

Joey: I'll be back tonight.

Joey looks at the assembled team, nods and addresses them.

Joey: Are you guys ready?

The birds nod their heads, still with an angry and determined look on their face.

Joey: Ok, then follow me!

Joey and the birds fly off into the sky, Joey leads the way. After a quick flight to the bay, Joey lands onto the bay dock. Sandy has just come back from fishing and hugs Joey with excitement. There are buckets of fish on the dock. It looks like yet another good day. Sandy then looks at the birds who have also landed on the dock. They still have that mean determined look on their faces.

Sandy: Um, Joey. Who are they?

Joey: Yeah, Um about that. I have a favor to ask. Would you teach them, what I taught you? You know, about fishing and getting water. We are rebuilding in the city, and they need a teacher.

Sandy: Ok, but I've heard that falcons and crows at times eat seagulls. Will we be alright? (She whispers).

They both look at the birds and they still have that determined scary look on their faces. Joey looks back at sandy, then says with a questionable expression.

Joey: Yea, I think we will be alright.

Sandy: Ok, if you say so.

Sandy looks at the birds and addresses them with a strict tone.

Sandy: Alright everyone, it's time to learn how to fish. Follow me!

Joey stays on the dock and watches as Sandy flies around and teaches the birds, how to fish. She is strict but helpful. The birds struggle at first, but then start to get the hang on it. She teaches them how to circle and grab the fish. Some use their mouths and others use their claws. As Joey looks on, an expression of pride comes to him on how far Sandy has evolved. Joey doesn't need to help; he has taught Sandy well. Sandy flashes Joey a smile from a distance. The student has now become the teacher.

As the birds continue to fish, Sandy lands on the dock to speak with Joey.

Sandy: They look like they are getting the hang of it. I can't believe you got everyone to work together.

Joey: Yeah, I'm surprised to, but it's working. Listen Sandy, I need to go back to the city for the night. I need to sort some things out. Can you continue to teach them everything I taught you, and then show them the water source. I'm going to take some fish and water for the others.

Sandy: Yeah sure, just do me favor. Be careful, I don't know what I'd do without you.

Joey: I will Sandy, I will.

Joey hugs Sandy and all the birds turn to look. They all make a mocking woo sound at Joey and Sandy. Joey blushes and then addresses the birds.

Joey: Alright, Alright! Hey everyone, I'm heading back to the city. Remember now, Sandy is the boss. She will teach you everything you need to know.

Joey fills up his backpack with fish and waters and takes off. He is headed back to the city. The day has gone by so fast. It's late afternoon. He is tired, a lot has been done today; but there is still more to be done.

As he gets back to the parking lot structure and all the birds are on the penthouse. Joey looks down at the rooftop and sees that all the materials gathered have been broken and scattered. From the sky there is a bunch of broken sticks and cleaning supplies that spell out the words STOP! Joey is shocked and exasperated at the scene. He then looks over at the penthouse where the sign was hanging. It's now on the floor split into the middle in two pieces. Joey flies to the penthouse where Freddy and Larry were standing. He addresses them with some anger.

Joey: What happened!

Larry: The rats came, they started attacking us. When we flew off, they started breaking all the materials we gathered.

Freddy: They were ready to get violent. They didn't say anything, they just came in and started fighting.

Joey looks at some of the birds and sees some scratches on some of them. He then sighs. He never wanted this to be something that would cause a war. He was just trying to make life better for everyone.

Joey: I'm sorry everyone, I should have spoken with the rats beforehand. This is my fault. Is everyone ok?

Freddy: Yes, but they are scared. They do not want to continue until they get some reassurance that the rats will not attack again.

Joey: I'll talk to the rats now. Tell everyone to stand by.

Joey looks at the scared faces of many of the birds and then goes down to the penthouse door. He opens it and then begins to walk in. He still has his backpack on. It's time to speak with the rats.

Chapter Seventeen: The Rat Pack

Joey makes his way down to the basement. It's so dark that he needs to hold the sides with his wings as he slowly descends. The door is slightly open. He slowly pushes it open and sees some dim light. As he opens it a rat approaches him and gets right in his face. "What do you want?" the rat says with anger. The rat is trying to pick a fight.

Joey looks him right in the eyes and with intimidating confidence replies, "I want to speak with whoever is in charge."

The rat gives a devious smile and replies, "Right this way Joey." Joey is confused that the rat knows his name and gives an inquisitive look. He follows the rat down the hallway. The rat is very large and has hairs sticking up from the back of his neck.

As Joey goes down the hallway, he sees that the area is lit with torches around the walls. There are dozens of rats just sitting around, all looking at him with hostility as Joey walks by. They are smaller than the one who is guiding him. As he continues to walk, he sees scattered materials that must have been gathered from the trash. They are piled up. The rats look like they are hoarding materials but not using them for anything. Then he looks up at the ceiling, there's a bunch of rusty ventilation equipment going in all directions.

Joey enters the main area of the basement and sees an open room. Again, this room is lit with torches and debris. Straight ahead of Joey is a small desk with three rats. One rat is sitting by the desk, similar to how Joey's father would sit at his office. This rat is also much larger, like the one guiding him through the basement. He also has hairs raised above his neck. The other two rats are standing behind him, they are smaller but still intimidating. They all have an evil smile on their face. Joey walks to desk to address the rats. He is scared but does not want to show it. He then addresses the rats.

Joey: Hello, my name is Joey. I think you might already know that though.

Frank: Aw Joey, yes, my name is Frank. Behind me is Sammy and Dean. We are the leaders of the rat pack. Why are you gracing us with your presence?

Joey: I've come to ask for a truce between the rats and the other animals. We are trying to work together, to make life better for all animals. We would like for you to be a part of it.

Frank: A truce? Work together? Rat's work alone.

Joey: I understand this idea might be unique, but if we work together; we can all survive easier. I understand you control the trash, but what about fresh fish and water? Wouldn't you like to barter for other basic survival needs?

Frank: The idea is not unique; I've heard it before. The rats get by just fine. What could you possibly offer us?

Joey pulls off his backpack and dumps the waters and fish on the desk. Dean and Sammy's eyes widen. Frank gives the same evil smile he has been giving since the start. Sammy and Dean quickly grab the fish and waters off the desk. They place them behind Frank.

Frank: That's a lot of food and water. You are just going to give it to us?

Joey: Yes, and more to come. We would like to work with you. To make things better for everyone involved.

Frank: Ok, tell you what. Tomorrow, deliver us more fish and water. We will discuss what we can do for everyone else. To make things better.

Joey: Sounds great, I'll be back tomorrow. In the meantime, we will continue to rebuild.

Frank: Sounds like another great plan Joey. Dean, Sammy is this ok with you?

Sammy: Sounds like a plan boss. He's bringing us treats. The Candyman.

Dean: Yeah, I'll be standing in the corner. Waiting for Joey to come back.

Frank: Alright Joey, we will try this out. Perhaps we don't do it my way.

Joey: Ok, I'll be back tomorrow.

Joey walks away and is guided by the same rat who was standing by the door. As he exits, the rat looks at him and says with now a friendly smile, "Good Luck!"

The door creeks behind him, while remaining slightly open. Joey pushes the door open a little and again the rat gets in his face. "What do you want!"

Joey: What's your name?

Damien: Damien, I am the gatekeeper and enforcer. (He says with a smile) I'll be seeing you again Joey. Good Luck!

Damien then closes the door. Staring deviously at joey until it closes. Joey slowly walks up the poorly lit stairs and back up to the penthouse. It is evening now. The birds are all resting on top of the penthouse and high parapets. Joey flies back to the penthouse to address Freddy and Larry.

Larry: How did it go? Were you able to make a deal with them?

Joey: I think so. I'm bringing them fish tomorrow. We can start rebuilding tomorrow.

Larry: I don't think we can trust them.

Freddy: We will see how it goes. I also have my doubts.

Joey: Yes, we must try.

Joey finds a spot on the penthouse and immediately falls asleep. He is exhausted. This time he doesn't hear the noise from the city. There is too much noise in his head for the outside distractions to bother him.

The next morning Joey wakes to everyone cheerful. The birds have come back with buckets that are filled with food and water. It's a morning feast, Joey meets them to join. The spirits of everyone are high, they all eat and drink as the sun comes up. It's another hot and dry day.

Joey begins to grab a few fish and waters and put them into his backpack. The other birds look at him. They start to mutter to each other. Kevin addresses Joey.

Kevin: What are you doing, Joey? That fish is for all of us.

Joey: I must bring some to the rats. It's part of the deal.

Kevin: A deal with the rats. The ones who destroyed our shelter project and sign. They should get nothing.

Joyce: Yeah, I agree with Kevin.

Joey sighs and addresses everyone. He understands the others being skeptical.

Joey: Look we need materials from the trash. The humans throw away a lot of useful food and materials. One man's trash, is another animal's treasure. We also must keep the peace.

Kevin: Keep the peace! Look what they did!

Larry: That's enough Kevin, Joey knows what he's doing. We need to try.

Kevin storms off with anger. Larry looks at Joey, then walks with him away from the others.

Larry: I'll talk to everyone. Go back down, try to reason with the rats.

Joey nods his head at Larry. Then he looks up at the penthouse. Freddy placed a new plywood with the writings of Joey's previous list. He then flies over to Larry and Joey.

Freddy: I'll send the birds for more food and water. I'll also make sure everyone is ready to rebuild. You do your best to reason with the rats.

Joey: Thanks Freddy, I'll be back.

Joey begins to walk down the stairs again with his backpack firmly secured on his body. He gets to the door of the basement. Again, it is slightly opened. Joey begins to open the door, and yet again Damien gets in Joeys face. He has a look like he is going to kill Joey. Joey does not back down, he smiles right back Damien.

Joey: Take me to Frank.

Damien: You got it, Boss.

Joey: What's up with the crazy looks and intimidation?

Damien: Just keeping you honest, Joey.

Joey: Yeah well, do your job and take me to Frank.

Damien: As you wish, Boss.

Joey: Stop calling me that!

Damien smiles and says, "Follow me.... Boss." Joey is irritated at the intimidation. As he walks through the hall, he hears snide comments and whispers from the rats. They are all making comments about him. He gets to the main part of the basement. The leaders of the rat pack are all at the desk again. It's as though they never moved from the last time. Joey takes his backpack and dumps the waters and fish on the desk.

Joey: Here you go, enjoy! Now, let's talk about working together.

Sammy and Dean quickly take the fish and water and put it behind Frank. Frank is again smiling with an evil grin. Sammy and Dean go to the other side of the desk and stand just to the side of Joey so he can't look at all of them at the same time. Joey turns to look at one of them, then the other, then he looks straight at Frank.

Joey: So are we going to talk about working together? I brought you some food and waters.

Frank: What food and water?

Joey: The food and water I just brought you now, and yesterday.

Frank: I don't know what you are talking about, Boss. Sammy? Dean? You know of this?

Sammy: Nope don't know what he is talking about.

Dean: Doesn't ring a bell, Frank.

Joey is frustrated, he knows they are playing games. This has become a more difficult situation than he anticipated. He addresses Frank with some anger.

Joey: So, it's going to be like that, huh?

Frank: I'm afraid so.... Boss. That's Life.

Joey: What do you have against working together to make it easier on everyone?

Frank starts pacing back and forth behind the desk. As he looks to the side, Joey notices a long scar along the back on his ear and the back of his head. He is surprised that he didn't notice it before. The hairs on his neck are still straight up, like Damien's.

Frank: Joey, where are you from?

Joey: I'm from a beach, south of here. Why?

Frank: That sounds nice. You see, I am from here. Been here all my life. It wasn't always in this abandoned parking lot basement though. I come from the sewers. I am a sewer rat. There is a sewer cap at the corner of this parking lot. One day it was open, and I crawled out. The sewer is a very difficult place to grow up. It is a living hell. Nobody works together. It's kill or be killed. I've lived a long time, and the key to survival is to fight for everything and expect nothing from nobody. The only way I have survived, is I did it my way.

Joey: That's not the best way. There is a better way.

Frank: There isn't Joey. It's been tried before. Other animals, even seagulls have tried and failed. It's best to stick with your own kind and survive as you can. We will continue to do this and stop anyone who gets in our way. And our way, is my way.

Joey: If that's the case, then we will work together without you. We will go through the trash, though. That's not for just the rats. Do you understand that?

Frank: Every action has its consequences. Goodbye Joey.

Joey: But...

Frank: Goodbye Joey, Damien escort Joey out of here.

Dean and Sammy both get close to Joey. They whisper in each ear, "it's time to leave."

Dean: Ain't that a kick in the head.

Sammy: You got too close for comfort.

Damien aggressively grabs Joey by the shoulder and pulls him. He picks him up and carry's him to the door. The other rats are again whispering snide comments as he is caried out. Damien throws Joey outside the door and gives him one last evil, grinning look.

Damien: I hope to see you again, Boss.

The door slowly closes shut. Again, not completely shut. Joey stands up with anger. He takes a step closer to the door to open it, but then thinks twice. He dusts himself off and walks back up the stairs. This is going to be harder than he expected.

Joey walks up the stairs and onto the rooftop. The birds are again putting together shelters. Joey is astonished at the determination of the crew. It's a shame that he must tell them what happened. Larry flies over to get the scoop on what went on in the basement. He sees Joey's face and knows it didn't go well.

Larry: Joey, do I have to ask.

Joey: Not well, I don't think they will listen. The leader Frank, he is stubborn. Maybe we should put a hold on gathering materials and building the shelters.

Larry: No, the hell with them. We got everyone on board. How many are there?

Joey: There's a lot. I couldn't count, and it was dark. They have enough to make it a war.

Larry: We have our fair share as well. Also, word has gotten out. There's been interest from other animals, both big and small. Your idea is spreading through the city. You brought us the idea, if we must fight for it; we will fight for it.

Joey: Just give me some time to think about this. There has got to be a civil way to solve this issue. Violence cannot be the answer. I want peace, not war.

Larry: Sometimes war can result in peace.

Joey: Just, give me some time to think about what the next move is. I'm going to head to the bay. I'll be back tomorrow with some food and water for everyone. Please, in the meantime. Do not go through the trash. It might cause more violence.

Larry: What did they do to you? Beat you up, throw you out and shut the door.

Joey: Pretty much. Well, the door stayed open. I think they might be afraid of it locking them in.

Larry: Yeah, this is an old building. Doors tend to stick together sometimes. Everything's boarded up, it has been vacant for years.

Joey: I know, it would make for a perfect shelter for hundreds. If only we didn't have to worry about the rats.

Larry: Yeah, we can't leave. I'll talk to Freddy. You go clear your head.

Joey takes off into the sky and heads to the bay. His mind is racing the whole way back. He flies onto the dock and immediately on the boat where he sits down and meditates. What is he going to do about the rats? He doesn't want a war, but the rats are not budging. Is there a way he can persuade them to work together with everyone else?

Sandy comes back from fishing. She again has caught a lot of fish; the falcons and crows have headed back with food for other animals. She investigates the boat to and sees Joey. He's never not greeted her immediately when she flies in. He is sitting on one of the seats looking at the ocean. He looks to be in a troubled state and very distant.

Sandy: Joey, hey are you alright?

Joey: Yeah, fine.

Sandy: It looks like somethings wrong.

Joey: Uh, it was a rough day. The rats at the parking lot. They got physical and do not want to work together.

Sandy: Oh, well you knew you would get some resistance.

Joey: Yes, but it might be more than we can handle, it might get physical.

Sandy: Would you like me to come and help?

Joey: No, it's too dangerous.

Sandy: Too dangerous? Listen, you have taught me a lot; but I have been on my own for a long time. In and around the city my whole life. I probably know more about the city than you do. I appreciate the skills you taught me, but don't think you are protecting me. I am a survivor, regardless of the circumstances.

Joey: Listen, I'm sorry. I care about you. I don't want anything to happen to you. Can we just leave it alone for now? I'm going to go for a walk. It's been a really rough day.

Sandy: Fine, but I'd like to talk more about it later.

Joey: We will, I just need to figure out a plan. I need to be alone for a bit, go for a walk.

Joey walks away. Sandy is very concerned but lets him walk away. Joey goes to the end of the dock. He sighs and looks ahead. There is a head peeking from behind the tree gazing at him. Joey looks over and the head of the creature quickly hides behind the tree. Joey acts like he didn't see the head. He starts to casually whistle and walk around in circles in a nonchalant way. Then when the head peeks out again, he flies around the other side of the tree, so the head can't see him. He approaches the tree and sees who it is. It's Speedy, but he doesn't see Joey quite yet. Joey runs real fast at the tree. "Peek-a-boo, I see you!" Speedy turns around and with a startled look and says, "Aw you got me."

Joey: Are you spying on me, Speedy?

Speedy: Um, maybe. Orders from your father to check in on you from time to time. I'm just doing my job Joey! (He says in his usually high-strung way).

Joey: Yeah, I figured he might do that at some point.

Speedy: Looks like you have yourself in a predicament. Do you need help?

Joey: No, I need to do this myself. Please, do not tell anyone; I don't want to get anyone else involved.

Speedy: I can't do that Joey. My orders are to observe and report.

Joey: Ugh, just say I'm fine. It hasn't gotten out of control yet.

Speedy: Joey, you should come home. Everyone misses you.

Joey: I can't. I need to help everyone. Show them what my father taught me.

Speedy: I'll sugar coat it, but you need to be careful. Change is not for everyone.

Joey: I will Speedy. Are you going to check up on me again.

Speedy: What do you think?

Joey: Alright, fine. Next time, don't hide. Come and say hello, I'll give you some fish and water.

Speedy: Can I meet the pretty lady next time?

Joey smiles and bashfully nods his head yes. Speedy smiles and says, "Well, I'm off." He then runs really fast back to Bro Beach. Joey sighs, he is still thinking of what needs to be done. He flies up into the tree and watches the sunset. "It can be done, we can all work together," Joey says while nodding off into the tree.

Chapter Eighteen: A Speedy Tale

Speedy runs real fast along the coast. He gets to the office of Don Gull. Breathing very heavy he says to Don Gull, "Joey is in trouble, he's got a conflict with the rats." Don gull sighs and puts his wing to his face, "Meet me for dinner at my place." Speedy salutes Don, putting his wing to his eyebrow, "You got it, sir."

The evening comes and Speedy arrives at the house. Don and Theresa are sitting at the table. A table setting is already waiting for Speedy. Speedy, looks at the table and then looks at Theresa. "We need one more place setting for the table," Speedy says with sincerity. Don and Theresa look at each other with confusion. Suddenly, Tony walks in and there is an awkward silence. Theresa is stunned, she hasn't talked to her younger brother in a long time. He looks at Theresa and with a half-smile then addresses Theresa.

Tony: Hi, Theresa. It's been a while. I've missed you.

Theresa: It sure has.

Theresa hugs Tony, Don and Speedy both smile. They have grown apart over the years. Theresa instructs Tony to sit down. He sits at the table and at first there is silence. Then Speedy speaks up.

Speedy: I had to tell Tony.

Theresa: Thank you Speedy. So is my baby in trouble.

Speedy acts out what he saw in a very fast manner. Telling the story of the rats and the resistance. They all listen. Then Don Gull, addresses everyone.

Don Gull: Ugh, he's a bright boy. He can be stubborn at times. We will need to check up on him more.

Speedy: I can do that! I don't mind at all.

Don Gull: Thank you Speedy.

Tony: He's a bright and resourceful kid. He will be alright. I understand what he's going through.

Theresa: Yeah, but we don't want what happened to you, happen to Joey. There is silence at the table and Tony stands up.

Tony: Theresa, I'm sorry. I'm sorry I left. Can we bury this quarrel.

Theresa: Yes, I miss you. I just worry about our son. He is a lot like you in so many ways. A lot like Don too. What I love about you guys is also what I fear.

Don Gull: Everyone in this world needs to find their own way. It doesn't always line up with others. I worry for my son, but he needs to sort things out on his own. He has gotten into to a conflict. Anyone who goes through life with no conflict, has not challenged the world.

Speedy: Well-spoken Don! (Speedy says quickly while raising his wings and everyone shakes their head with a smile).

There is a silence after the speedy remarks. They start eating dinner. Tony has a few bites and gives Theresa a look.

Tony: I miss these home cooked meals. Theresa, it's just like mom made.

Theresa smiles at Tony. They continue to eat. Don looks up after a few bites and looks at everyone.

Don Gull: This is nice. Tony, come for dinner more often.

Tony smiles and then looks at Theresa. Theresa nods at Tony and gives a content expression. They continue eating dinner.

Chapter Nineteen: The Conflict

Joey wakes up in the tree. He slept there all night. He goes back to the Boat. Sandy is fast asleep. He grabs a fish and water and places it next to Sandy. Then he begins to pack his backpack. The waters and fish fall out as soon as he picks it up. There is a hole in it, the rats must have torn it. Joey is angry, that's the backpack his mother gave him. He paces back and forth in a fit of rage. Then he eats a few fish and drinks some water. It's warm and dry and he foresees a long day. He leaves the backpack and flies off into the sky for the city. He's angry muttering to himself the whole trip.

As he lands on the parking lot structure, he notices the huts that the birds have built. Kevin and Joyce are instructing all the other birds. Larry is sitting with Freddy at the top of the penthouse looking over everything. Joey flies over to greet them.

Joey: This looks great, are the rats ok with this?

Larry: The rats won't be a problem.

Joey: Wait, what do you mean by that?

Larry: The door, we shut it. Then we blocked it with some heavy cinderblocks we found. It took a lot of birds to do it, but we got it done.

Joey: If they can't get out, won't they die?

Larry: Not sure, but they won't bother us now. They deserve this.

Joey: Freddy did you allow this?

Freddy: Larry was set on this. I do not agree with how we did it, but something needed to be done.

Joey: This isn't right guys, there must be a better way.

Larry: Freddy and I have dealt with the rats for a very long time. Enough is enough. You were right, it's time for a change.

Joey: What if they get out? It will be an all-out war?

Larry: I've seen this happen before. It's time for a change. I am willing to die for it, if I must. The future should be to work together and not in fear.

Freddy: Joey, this has happened before. This time will be different. The rats have been controlling the city and making things worse for everyone. Look at this city, the rats have intimidated and beaten anyone who gets in their way. I don't like it, but it's time to fight back.

Joey, very frustrated; starts to think. What if the rats do get out, and if they don't; will they just let them die? Then he thinks, the ventilation equipment. If they could open that, they would get out.

Joey: Guys, the vents. There are vents in the basement.

Freddy and Larry look with a wide-eyed gaze. Suddenly the rats appear moving fast. Everyone is still working on the huts. Joey yells, "Everyone fly away!"

The rats run at the birds, and they fly off. Kevin is inside one of the huts, and Damien approaches with an evil gaze. Larry flies to the hut and rams hard right into Damien knocking him back. He then approaches Kevin, "get out son!" He pulls Kevin out of the hut and Damien gets back on his feet. He pushes the hut over the edge of the rooftop with Larry still inside.

Damien: I hate pigeons. (He says with an evil smile).

The hut falls off the rooftop. Joey flies to try and catch Larry but he is stuck inside. It falls to the ground with Larry inside. A shocked and terrified look comes to Joey as he slows down and realizes he can't save him. Kevin is flying next to Joey and has a look of terror on his face.

The other rats are breaking the huts and throwing them off the rooftop. All the other birds are safe on the penthouse or flying around. Damien looks up at Freddy and smiles. Freddy in anger looks at a few of the other flacons and says, "Attack!"

The falcons swarm around the rats and Freddy heads straight for Damien. Freddy and two other falcons grab Damien and fly up in the sky. Damien is clawing at them. The two other falcons let go, Freddy is struggling carrying Damien. He continues to swipe at Freddy. "You will never win!" Damien says with an evil stare. Then he swipes Freddy right in the face. Freddy lets go of Damien and he starts to fall. His momentum has him land on the adjacent lower rooftop and he rolls around. Damien falls straight down, landing on the sewer cap next to the parking lot. Damien is dead. Not far from him, is the hut with Larry inside.

Suddenly, a voice yells from the other side of the rooftop. Frank is standing with Sammy and Dean.

Frank: Retreat!

Frank has an evil look on his face while Dean and Sammy looked shocked. The rats go down the stairs to the second level. Joey goes down to check on Larry. It's bad, very bad. Larry is crushed by the hut and the fall. Kevin and Joyce come down to see Larry as well. Suddenly, Larry opens his eyes. He looks at Kevin and Joey. He knows this is the end.

Larry: Don't stop the fight, this time we will win. Son, you and Joyce; I love you both.

Larry closes his eyes and fades off. Tears run down Kevin and Joyce's face. Kevin looks in shock. Joey looks at Kevin.

Joey: I'm sorry. Kevin, Joyce, I'll give you some time with him.

Joey then flies over to Freddy. He is on his back with his eyes closed. A few of the falcons are standing in a circle surrounding Freddy. Joey takes his wing and pats his chest, "Freddy, you ok?" Suddenly, Freddy takes a huge gasp, opens his eyes and sits up. Joey and the others show an expression of relief. Freddy looks up confused for a second and then looks straight at Joey.

Freddy: Larry, is he ok?

Joey: Larry is dead.

Freddy shakes his head and then slowly gets up. He dusts himself off. He looks at everyone with a sad look. He puts his wing to his head, then covers his face.

Freddy: I need to be alone for a while. I can't do this right now.

Freddy flies off in the opposite direction of the parking lot rooftop. His flight pattern is wabbly, he is clearly injured. Many of the other birds fly over towards Joey. They look at Joey, looking for guidance. Joey sticks out his chest, looks at everyone.

Joey: We need to fight for change, it's our only choice now.

Chapter Twenty: The Dilemma

The day turns into night and Joey and the others are standing on the lower rooftop across the street from the parking lot. Kevin is in the corner angry at his father's passing. Joyce is next to him trying to console him. A few falcons and crows fly over with some food and water. Joey brings the food and water over to Kevin.

Joey: Um, hey Kevin, Joyce. I brought you some food and water.

Kevin: I'm not hungry.

Joyce: Yeah, me either.

Joey: Listen, I'm sorry what happened to your father. He was a good bird.

Kevin: Yeah, it should have been me. He saved me.

Joey: He didn't fight for nothing. We will fight for a better tomorrow. You will get over this feeling.

Kevin: I can't feel anything. I'm angry at the world, and I know I can't change it. I'd rather be dead than live with this guilt.

Joyce: Don 't be saying that, Kevin.

Kevin: I mean it, it's not fair.

Joey: We need you Kevin, the way you instructed the other birds. That will come in handy when we rebuild.

Kevin: Will we rebuild, will the rats let us?

Joey: We will find a way; I'll make sure of that.

Joey walks away with a somber look. Then he looks at the other birds. They all have a defeated look on their faces. Joey needs to address it.

Joey: Listen everyone, I know we are feeling defeated right now. Everything is going against us. We will overcome this; we will prevail over the rats. We must fight for a better tomorrow.

Kevin walks over, he's a little more coherent now. He looks at Joey.

Kevin: Are you leaving for the bay?

Joey thinks for a second and realizes they need a leader to overcome this dilemma.

Joey: I will not leave, until we overcome this; and we will overcome this.

All the other birds nod their heads somberly. Everyone settles in for the night. A few crows are on the lookout for a possible invasion.

The next morning Joey wakes to Joyce yelling, "Everyone, look." It's the rats on the ground, they are opening the sewer cap where Damien had fallen to his death. They open the sewer cap and pick up Damien's body. Frank looks straight up at the birds and grins. Damien's body goes into the sewer. The rats then walk away leaving the sewer cap open. As the birds look on, Frank comes back holding something. It's a yellow backpack. Sandys backpack. He looks up at Joey and yells.

Frank: We need to talk!

Joey is in shock. They have Sandy. He looks down at Frank and nods his head. Frank then slowly walks away, he does a little dance with the backpack, twirling it around, as if he is mocking Joey. Joey's face turns to anger, and he walks away from the edge.

Joey: They have Sandy! I must meet with them.

Kevin approaches Joey.

Kevin: I will come with you. I can't let what happened to me, happen to you.

Joey: No, I don't want anyone else to get hurt.

Kevin: No Joey, we work together; you taught us that.

Joey looks at the other birds as they circle around him. He realizes this is no longer a team. This is part of his family now. He realizes now for better or worse, this family will stay together.

Joey: Alright, I need a team to meet with the rats. Who wants to come with me?

Joyce: Me!

Kevin: You know I'm in.

A few of the falcons raise their wings. One of them yells, "We have your back."

Joey: Alright it's settled; let's go.

The team flies back to the parking lot and then stops at the ramp that goes down to the lower level. They slowly walk down to the lower-level parking lot.

It's dark but light shines through the open sides, the ones that are not boarded up. Some of it is boarded up, but not well. They walk down and see an army of rats, dozens of them. Frank is in front, behind him as always are Sammy and Dean. They have a concerned look on their faces. Joey looks down and right next to Frank is Sandy. She is tied up with wire on the ground. Then Joey yells to Sandy.

Joey: Sandy! Are you ok.

Sandy: Yes, I came to see you! They grabbed me on the rooftop.

Frank: Looks like I have the upper hand, Joey. Talk to me, Joey.

Joey approaches the rats and stands roughly ten feet away from them. Joyce and Kevin are by his side. The falcons are behind them with a determined look as always, ready to strike.

Joey: What do you want.

Frank: I want you, Joey. These radical ideas of change need to stop. It's over, it doesn't work. It never has worked.

Joey: We can work together Frank. It can be better for everyone.

Frank: A while back another bird said that to me, and you know what I did. I scratched his eye out. Him and his little bat friend, they never came back.

Suddenly Joey realizes, the seagull they are talking about is his uncle Tony. Was the bat Bert? Joey looks at frank with a wide eye gaze.

Joey: Tony and Bert?

Frank: Yeah, I think that was their names. They tried to work together, and I stopped them. I will now stop you as well.

Joey looks at Sandy, she has a terrified look on her face. He then looks at Frank with anger and yells.

Joey: Take me, I'm the one you want.

Frank thinks for a minute and grins back.

Frank: Ok, Joey it's a deal. Sammy grab Joey, Dean untie the seagull and bring her to the birds.

As they do the exchange thunder roars and it starts to rain. It hasn't rained in a long time. The exchange is made, and Joey is still standing but now tied up. Frank addresses everyone.

Frank: Now everyone let's go to the rooftop.

Chapter Twenty-one:
The Sewer

They slowly walk up to the rooftop, all the other birds are perched on the parapet watching. Rain is coming down, and flashes of lightning can be seen. They go to the corner of the rooftop. Right below is the open sewer. Frank yells loudly so everyone can hear them.

Frank: So, this is what's going to happen. When we have radical ideas, you will be thrown into the sewer. Joey will be the example.

Sammy and Dean are holding Joey. They have a confused look on their face.

Sammy: Frank, this is a bit much isn't it.

Dean: Yeh boss, are we sure we want to do this.

Frank gets angry and yells.

Frank: You two did not grow up in a sewer like I did. Maybe you should go in as well. Soon, more sewer rats will rise and take over the city. We will rise above and have it all to ourselves. If you won't throw him in, I will. Anyone who dares to stop me, will be killed.

The other birds are watching, waiting to strike. Joey looks and realizes this will be an all-out war. His new family, many could die. He needs to do something, but what? He is tied up. What can he do? Suddenly he gets an idea, play dead.

Joey falls to the ground as Frank approaches him. Frank looks at him on the ground. Lightning strikes in the background, startingly many. Sandy yells, "Joey!"

Frank: What happened?

Sammy: I don't know, maybe he had a heart attack.

Frank: Well, that's unfortunate. I knew he couldn't cut it in the city. I wanted to see his fear as he fell into the sewer. Anyways, he will still make for a nice dinner for the sewer rats.

Frank approaches Joey. Joey then opens his eyes. Frank looks at him surprised.

Frank: You're alive?

Joey: Yep, playing dead. (He says with a smile).

Joey then kicks with both feet up at Franks chest pushing him back. The birds then attack the rats. Swarming around them, causing chaos. Sandy and Kevin come to the rescue of Joey and untie him. Frank gets up, the hairs on his back are strait up with anger. He stands up showing his claws.

Frank: I'm going to kill you, Joey!

Joey gets untied and sits up. Sandy and Kevin look at him. Sandy pulls him up.

Sandy: We won't leave you!

Frank starts to approach them and suddenly in the distance he hears a loud shout. "Frank!!" Everyone stops fighting and gazes at the penthouse. Sitting on it, is Tony with a mean grin on his face. Frank stops charging and looks in terror.

Frank: Tony! (He says with a surprised grimace).

Tony soars over and starts fighting with Frank. Frank knocks him down. Joey comes over and knocks Frank from behind. Frank gets up and starts to charge after Joey, but as he charges Tony gets up. He flies over and grabs Frank picking him up with his claws. The rain is coming down hard. Tony flies pass the rooftop and struggles to fly. Frank is holding on to him.

Frank: If I go down, you go down with me.

Tony: I don't think so. An eye for an eye. (Tony looks at him and says with a struggling scream).

Tony pecks at one of Franks eyes. Frank immediately reacts by holding his hands to his eye. He releases his grasp of Tony and falls. While he falls, with one good eye, and the other still being covered with a hand. He stares straight at Tony, with an evil look all the way down. He falls straight into the sewer.

Tony struggles, but flies back onto the rooftop. Some of the rats look on in disbelief but stick around. The other rats scatter away. Joey looks at the falcons and crows. "The sewer cap, we need to close it," Joey says with determination. The Falcons and crows fly down and grab the sewer cap. With a struggle they place it back on the sewer manhole. They then fly back to the rooftop.

Everyone looks at the other rats who are still standing in disbelief. Sammy and Dean look at Joey in fear. Joey gets in between the rats and the birds and shouts.

Joey: If you want to stay, you can stay and join us. Otherwise leave.

Some of the rats stay, and a few more rats scatter off. Everyone left forms a half circle around Joey. To his right is Kevin and Joyce, to his left is Sandy and Tony. The rain stops, and there is a peak of sunlight. A silence comes over everyone. Sammy the rat yells out, with Dean by his side.

Sammy: So, what do we do now?

Joey looks over to Tony. He looks right back at him, and with a grin nods. Sandy gets close to Joey and holds his wing. Joey then looks over to everyone and says loudly: "We work together and rebuild!"

www.ingramcontent.com/pod-product-compliance
Lightning Source LLC
Chambersburg PA
CBHW052100150726
48002CB00002B/973